WALLY'S TOUCH

J. RICHARD MOORE

ISBN 978-1-962363-50-1 (Paperback)
ISBN 978-1-962363-51-8 (Ebook)

Inquiries and Book Orders should be addressed to:

Leavitt Peak Press
17901 Pioneer Blvd Ste L #298, Artesia, California 90701
Phone #: 2092191548

CHAPTER 1

"Wally, wake up! His wife exclaimed. Can't you hear the phone?"

"What…who…I'm up. Oh, the phone," he answered in a sleepy mumble.

Wally collected his thoughts.

"Good evening, DeVere Funeral Home, Wally speaking." He said.

He heard a sweet voice say.

"Our mother has passed away in her sleep." Wally comforted her and said that he would be over at once.

"Come back to bed, honey. It's late and cold outside. Get back under the covers and keep me warm. I need your breath on the back of my neck. Call Vince to make the removal, "Wally's wife, Helen pleaded.

"Honey, we have gone over this again and again. You know that I am obligated to my families to make the removals. You know there is no place in this world I would rather be then next to you in our bed. This is the Miller family that owns the bank! Mrs. Miller was ninety-two and a very lovely, respected woman in the community," Wally said.

"I understand, Wally. Try not to wake the children and lock the door. I love you, Wally." Helen said with a smile.

Wally leaned over and kissed his wife. He got dressed and backed the suburban out of the garage. Helen was already sound asleep before he left the drive.

Wally and Helen had recently purchased the funeral home from William DeVere. William had built his life around his wife, Emily and the funeral home after she died Mr. Devere sold it to Wally.

William and his late wife planned to retire in Naples, Florida where they owned a home. His dreams were shattered by her sudden bout with cancer which drained the life out of her spirited body. Her death was too much for William. There was no way he could handle Emily's service. He called Wally, who was an energetic and respected funeral director. Wally worked for a firm in Goodland which was a small town thirty miles away from William's home. Wally's reputation was well known in the area because of the care he gave the families he served.

Wally came at once and graciously and lovingly took Mrs. DeVere into his care and performed a wonderful service. William could see and feel the passion Wally had for the funeral industry. The care that Wally took in dealing with the DeVere family and friends was apparent to all. The ceremony was a celebration of the life of a great and loved woman.

The next day, William called Wally and asked him to stop by the funeral home. He had something important to talk to him about.

When Wally arrived William said, "Please sit down Wally, I have a proposition for you and your family. I would like for you to purchase my funeral home."

Wally sat there for a moment in shock before he could answer. "Uh, Mr. DeVere, thank you so much for the offer; but I could not afford such a grand funeral home as yours."

The funeral home was built in 1893 and was a former Governor's home before his term. The home was a Grand Victorian with hardwood floors and ornate oak trim through out. The house also had two fireplaces and the most beautiful stained glass in the county. William added on a large chapel and built a garage that would hold five cars. William had a passion for landscaping and the grounds were immaculately groomed like a country club.

William looked at Wally and Said, "Wally, I see me forty years ago in your eyes and spirit. After the passing of Emily, I cannot conduct another funeral. I contacted Mr. Miller at the bank this morning and he is taking care of all of the arrangements. I have no children and I only have one request: that you say yes and that you take care of Emily's rose bushes that are planted around the entire funeral home."

Wally embraced William and thanked him for a dream opportunity.

Wally arrived at the Miller home before sunrise. There were several cars in the driveway and most of the lights in the home were on. Wally walked to the front door and rang the door bell.

Wally was dressed in a blue blazer, khaki cuffed pants, paisley wine colored tie and a charcoal cashmere topcoat. Wally was always conscious of his appearance in public. He wore a suit for the calling hours and the day of the funeral. He always wore a coat and tie for the removal of the family's loved one.

Mrs. Miller's granddaughter answered the door and Wally made her feel at ease right away while paying his respects and condolences.

"Are you Mrs. Miller's granddaughter?" he softly asked.

"Yes, I'm Rachel, her oldest," she answered in a sad voice.

"Well, I can see the beautiful resemblance of your grandmother in your eyes," Wally said with a smile.

Rachel just looked at him and said, "Thank you."

The family was all gathered in the formal living room. As Wally entered the room he glanced at everyone and said, "I am so sorry for your loss. Mrs. Miller was a truly loved woman. May I see her?"

Mrs. Miller's son Alfred stood up holding back the tears. "She is in her room, up the stairs and down the hall on the left."

"I will be happy to wait until you have said your goodbyes to her," Wally said in a soft voice.

Each and every member entered Mrs. Miller's room to see her at peace in her bed. This took two hours and Wally patiently waited. The family was so happy that he took the time and allowed them to spend time with her.

"Now if you don't mind, I will take Mrs. Miller into my care," Wally said to the family. The entire room seemed engulfed with pain and sorrow from the loss of their loved one. There was also a feeling of love and peace at the way Wally was handling the removal of their treasure from her home.

Wally quietly entered the room. Mrs. Miller's frail body lay on a beautiful carved cherry bed with a silk canopy. She was dressed in a long white linen nightgown, buttoned to the neck. A floral bedspread was draped over her lap.

Her eyes were closed as if in a deep peaceful sheep. Her snow white hair seemed to blend into the oversized feather pillow. She looked tiny in such a grand bed. Wally just stood there with his hands held together, gazing at Mrs. Miller's peaceful state.

Then he looked around the room. The walls were a rich melon color with a glorious border. A marble fireplace was on the north wall with the presence of a fire that had burned long ago. Many paintings hung on the walls and the windows were adorned with Italian lace.

Wally positioned his cot by the bed and lowered the bedspread with the utmost care. As Wally touched her frail hand, an amazing feeling surged throughout his body. He stood over her and gently placed his hand on hers and felt a goodness beyond any feeling he had ever experienced before. He closed his eyes and saw children in a horse drawn carriage going down a winding dirt road with a church off in the distance. The sky was a brilliant blue and the trees were as green as any seen in Augusta, Georgia. He could also hear the church bells and the children laughing. He then saw a young woman with lily white skin standing over a child in a classroom, lovingly helping the child read. Wally took a deep breath as the smell of freshly baked bread entered his lungs. The rich smell made him smile. He then saw a young couple walking up to a model T, hand in hand gazing into each other's eyes. These visions were so real to Wally that he could almost reach and touch the moment. He did not want this feeling to go away. Then he heard a knock at the door and he collected his thoughts.

"Wally, it's Rachel," a little voice said.

"Yes, dear…I'll only be a moment," Wally said as he gently lifted Mrs. Miller onto the cot.

"I was wondering if you have to cover her face when you take her, I just couldn't bare the thought of her face being covered," she said as tears flowed down her cheeks.

"Rachel, I will not cover her face here or at my funeral home if you do not want me to. We will leave her face exposed. OK?" Wally said in a soft quite voice.

Wally zipped the velvet body bag up to her chest and placed a silk scarf around her neck and zipped the bag to the scarf. She looked as if she were in a sleeping bag at camp.

Wally carefully moved Mrs. Miller out of her bedroom for the last time, down the hallway and carefully down the beautiful ornate staircase. As Wally got to the bottom of the staircase, he was wondering about the thoughts of Mrs. Miller's life as he touched her hand in the bedroom. He felt as if he had touched her very soul. He felt an inner peace with his experience. As Wally reached the large entry way, he again expressed his sorrow about the family's loss and reassured them that he would be very careful with their treasure. Wally scheduled a time for the family to make the arrangements at the funeral home.

Wally always felt sadness in his heart when he took the body out of the home. He knew how difficult it was for a family to see their loved one taken out of a home that they had loved in, laughed in, lived in and shared special moments with their family and friends in. Wally was sensitive to the fact that the person would never grace the home physically, but live on in spirit.

Wally carefully loaded Mrs. Miller's body into his suburban and headed back to the funeral home. He could not wait to share with his wife the experience he felt as he touched Mrs. Miller's hand. He was still overwhelmed with joy and happiness about the love he felt from this elderly lady and the experience of her past life.

As he entered his driveway, he raised the electric garage door and pulled in and closed the door behind him. Wally's previous employer had a detached garage. They would pull the vehicle into the garage and transport the cot on a sidewalk to the funeral home twenty yards away. Wally did not like this because, somebody was always around to see the covered body as it was moved. Wally could sense the discomfort that the people felt from the sight as did he.

At the funeral home, Wally could pull into the garage. Lower the garage door, remove the cot and take it up a ramp and into the prep room. He could do this unnoticed.

Wally took his time as with every body, preparing Mrs. Miller and embalming her body. He never worried about how long this process would take, every case was different. Wally knew how important it was to prepare the body before the service and he always did a meticulous service to each departed one. He was held in high esteem by each family.

It was 6:45a.m. Wally ran up the stairs to wake Helen.

"Honey, get up, you won't believe what happened at the Miller residence!" Wally said like a child on Christmas morning.

"Oh my God, you dropped Mrs. Miller on the floor," She said still not quite awake.

"You know that is not funny! No dear, I did not drop Mrs. Miller." He said.

That was always a fear Wally had. He even had nightmares that he dropped a body in front of the entire family.

"Helen look at me…when I touched Mrs. Miller's hand, I felt an indescribable feeling, a feeling of the life that this woman lived. I feel so at peace because I can truly say she is in a better place with her family and friends that have passed away. Helen, it is not so much what I saw, but what I felt," Wally said, slowing down to catch his breath.

He had a glow about him that Helen had never seen before.

"Are you serious, or is this a practical joke? Maybe you were still asleep when you removed Mrs. Miller from her home," Helen said in a chuckle.

"I have never been more awake or more alive than now. I love you and the kids so much it hurts," Wally said grabbing Helen as they tumbled on the bed. He stopped and looking into her eyes and gently kissed her.

"I know it sounds crazy, but I felt her life while I was in her room. I could hear children and I could smell fresh rolls baking. I felt as if I were in a bakery. Please believe me."

Helen looked at her husband who was her best friend and her rock and said…

"I do believe you, Wally. You are such a wonderful caring man. If anyone could feel such a feeling, it would be you."

"Let's go wake up the kids," Wally said as he darted into their boy's room.

Wally leaned over and kissed each of his sleeping boys on the forehead. Wally and Helen just stood there in the room, looking at their sons peacefully sleeping. Wally turned to Helen and began to weep with happiness and said…"I am truly blessed."

Chapter 2

Wally and Helen walked into the kitchen. "I'm ready for a big break-fast. I'll cook and you just sit at the table and look pretty," Wally said.

"That sounds great, but I'm not the one who has been up all night," Helen said.

"You know, I don't even feel a bit tired. I have all of this bottled up energy, I could just dance!" Wally stood in the middle of the room and did a silly little dance as the boys entered the kitchen.

"Is dad flipping out again?" Jeremy said with a yawn.

"Come over here, you little heifer, let's boogie," Wally yelled.

Jeremy looked at his father and said, "We don't boogie anymore dad, you have truly lost your mind." His little brother, Sammy, nodded his head and smiled.

Jeremy just turned sixteen and pretty much knows everything and will tell you so. He is a sophomore at a small high school. Gets straight A's and an average basketball player on the Junior Varsity team. Jeremy is madly in love with Tess who is in his class. It is a very funny part of a boy's life, one minute they can care less about girls, then pow…he wants to spend every minute with or thinking about them.

Sammy is the youngest and unlike Jeremy, he is an average student. He is also the best athlete in his class. He excels naturally at football, basketball and baseball. Baseball is his passion. He still sleeps with his first baseball glove. He says it helps his game.

Jeremy and Sammy are the joy of their parents' lives. They can be mischievous and ornery as most kids that age. But they are lit-tle well behaved angels when dad has a family, visitation or funeral. They know how serious their dad is about his job and reputation. They have grown to respect that.

Wally started to fry bacon and had the boys break the eggs into a mixing bowl.

"Boys, lets not have egg shells in the eggs this time, OK." Wally said with a grin. Helen got up and put biscuits in the oven. Breakfast was a family affair for them. It was a great way to start the day. The boys looked forward to the morning meal. They all filled their plates and sat down at the table and waited for Wally to say the blessing. Wally looked at his family with pride and thanked the Lord for life and the experiences that they shared. He asked God to bless his family, and watch over the Miller family in their time of need. Before the prayer ended he paused and said," Thank-You Lord," and smiled. Helen also smiled. The whole family said, "Amen" together.

"Dad, can I go over to Tess' house when basketball practice is over. We have a school project we are working on," Jeremy said.

"Right…you just want to go over to Tess' house to play kissy face!" Sammy said with a sneer.

"Shut up, stupid!" Jeremy fired back.

"Whoa!" Wally interrupted. "Please don't call your loving brother stupid. Why would you call your brother stupid…we don't use words like that, not do we?"

Jeremy looked at his dad and said," You called that casket salesman who always calls on you stupid to mommy.

The whole family burst out laughing.

"Let's finish breakfast so you won't be late for school." Helen said to change the subject.

The boys excused themselves from the table. Helen looked at Wally and asked him to describe what happened at the Miller home. Wally told her in detail every wonderful thing that he experienced while holding Mrs. Miller's hand.

"You know Wally, you tell me the funeral service is the celebration of life and every service should be tailor made for that particular family. When the Millers come to make the arrangements, I would ask questions about what you saw in your vision and see if they are true. And another thing, Mr. Funeral Director…," she said with a look of love in her eyes.

"Yes, Mrs. Funeral Director," Wally said with a boyish grin.

"I desperately love and adore you, even if you are a little warped and strange. Maybe that is why I do love you," she said with a laugh.

"Why don't you hold that thought and let's continue this conversation in the bedroom after the boys are off to school," Wally whispered.

"Oh Wally," Helen chuckled.

Just before the Miller family arrived, Helen baked a loaf of fresh bread and the aroma drifted throughout the funeral home. Helen always wanted to be with Wally when he greeted the family before they make the arrangements. She would insist on coffee, soft drinks or anything to make the family at ease throughout the grieving process.

In most communities, the funeral home is usually a beautiful structure, with well maintained and groomed grounds. It is also a place where no one really wants to visit. Just walking up to the door is hard and creepy for most. Wally knows this and tries to make a visit to his funeral home as pleasant as possible.

Shortly after 10:00a.m., the doorbell rang. Wally greeted the entire Miller family. Mrs. Miller's daughter, Kim arrived with her husband and children. Son, Alfred, wife and children also followed. There were twelve in all. As they entered the room, Kim stopped and started to weep. She looked at her husband and said, "Oh my God, do you smell bread baking."

Wally looked at her and said, "I hope the smell of my wife's bread doesn't bother you and your family.

Kim looked at Wally and said, "No, no… My mother had baked fresh bread every Sunday since I can remember. Alfred, do you remember that she made you and I little loaves? Everyone loved her bread." Wally just looked at Helen and smiled.

Wally escorted the family into his arrangement office. When they got settled, Helen asked if she could bring them anything. Mrs. Miller's youngest granddaughter asked for some of the homemade bread.

Kim looked at her daughter and said, "Honey, the bread is probably for their family."

Helen said, "Oh no, dear. I will be happy to bring you all some bread."

"Could my brother Alfred slice the bread? He always sliced Mom's before our family dinners," Kim said.

"I'll bring it right out," Helen said.

This was a moment not experienced by many funeral directors, a family feeling at peace. Wally told the family that he would like to know some important memories that the family members would share with him before he started the funeral arrangements. This usually calmed the families.

"Maybe you could tell me about her childhood to adulthood. How did she meet Mr. Miller?" Wally asked.

"I remember Grandma talking about horse and buggy rides with her brothers and sisters to church and the fun they had," Emily said with a smile.

"Remember when dad told the story about when he proposed to mom, in his model T," Kim laughed. "It was the only time that Dad's hands ever perspired, Mom told us. She said that he was so nervous. Oh, God, how I miss them," Kim said as she broke into tears.

Wally stood up and handed a box of tissues to Kim.

"Wasn't your mother a school teacher?" Wally asked.

"Why yes," Kim said still sniffling. "She taught reading at a one room school house before she met daddy. Remember she read us the novel <u>Little Women</u>."

Emily looked up at her aunt and said in a petite voice, "Grandma read <u>Little Women</u> to me four times!" Everyone in the room laughed.

Wally looked at the family through the arrangement process and helped them select a casket. After this, Wally walked the family to the door. Alfred embraced Wally and told him how wonderful he was to show so much love and compassion to a family that he hardly knew. Wally smiled and told Alfred that he felt he knew them through Mrs. Miller.

Helen wrapped the still warm bread in foil and gave it to the Miller family. Alfred asked if they could bring bread to the viewing. Helen smiled and said that she would be happy to bake the bread and let Alfred slice it. Alfred thanked her. When the Miller family left, Helen hugged Wally, and they both laughed and wept in each other's arms.

"Wally, I don't believe what I just saw," she said.

"I know Helen…I am overcome with joy because the Miller family experienced at peace in so many ways. I don't really understand what happened, but you know that I do love my profession." Wally said embracing his sweet wife.

The Miller funeral was a very large service. Over 2600 people paint their respects at the two day visitation. The funeral mass was also well attended. Wally and his staff handled the funeral to perfection. Every detail was elegant and beautifully orchestrated.

After the service, Alfred and Kim both expressed their thanks.

"I cannot tell you how happy we are with your service. You made the death of our mother a celebration of her life. We will never forget your kindness," Kim said wiping away the tears.

They both hugged Wally and left the funeral home.

Chapter 3

Wally sat in the leather Queen Anne chair in the front of the fireplace. He took a deep breath and smiled. Wally sat in comfort and felt pride in the service he had provided for the Miller Family. He thought about the touch of Mrs. Miller's hand and the experience of her life that he felt from that touch.

His eyes grew heavy with fatigue and he dozed off just as the phone rang.

The sound shocked Wally out of his cat nap. He hurried to the phone and answered, "Good afternoon, DeVere Funeral Home, Wally speaking."

"Hey, Wally…It's Sheriff Tucker. You'd better get over here. The God Damn Wilson Boy hung himself in his cell."

"Oh my Gosh Sheriff…I'll be right over," Wally said in disbelief.

The coroner just arrived and one good thing, the little bastard saved the tax payers a lot of money, see you here, Wally," Sheriff Tucker said with a chuckle.

"Helen, I have to go to the jail. The Wilson boy hung himself in his jail cell." Wally said gaining his composure.

"Oh, no…how horrible, I'll get your coat dear." Helen said as she left the room for the hall closet.

"Well Sheriff Tucker didn't think it was so terrible. The coroner has just arrived so this could take a while." Wally said as he kissed Helen and reached for the garage door.

Wally was greeted by the newspaper man as he walked into the jail. This is such a big story for such a little newspaper.

"Hey Wally, do you have any information on the Wilson boy?" Dick Straw, the newspaper editor asked.

"I'm sure you know more than I do Dick," Wally said.

Wally went to the information desk at the jail and the receptionist told him,

"Sheriff Tucker is expecting you Wally, you can go on back."

Dick Straw interrupted and said, "I'll go back with Wally." He was hoping to get a picture.

"You know better than that, Mr. Straw. You know the Sheriff does not want any press here!!! She sharply said.

Wally heard a bell and the steel entrance door to the inside opened. As he walked in, he shuttered as the door shut behind him.

Sheriff Tucker greeted him and said, "This way, Wally. I'll take you to the little prick." Sheriff laughed out loud.

Tyson Wilson was a twenty year old native of their little town. He had a rap sheet longer that Santa's Christmas list. Tyson was in and out of institutions and jails most of his teenage life.

His father worked at that local mill and was mean as hell. If you looked at Mr. Wilson wrong, he would crack you first then hit you again if you got blood on him. Tyson hated his father and when he was in school, he would go to class with bruises on his face and arms. He would never admit his father was beating the tar out of him, but everyone knew.

Tyson had done everything from petty theft to armed robbery before he was sixteen. There was a time when a social worker tried to rehabilitate Tyson and it looked as if he was changing. Then Tyson put the social worker in the hospital with a fractured skull.

Last summer Tyson was at a party and got very drunk. He was with Jenny Morgan, who was the local whore. After he left the party, he took her to an isolated area behind an old railroad bridge that had not been used for years. Tyson wanted to have sex but she refused. Tyson beat her up and raped her. He tied her nude body to the bridge and left her. She had a fractured skull that left her in a coma. Her body had several cuts and cigarette burns. She died in the hospital two weeks later.

A farmer found her tied to the bridge eighteen hours after Tyson left her. There were several beer cans and smoked cigarette butts at the crime scene. The police found out that Tyson was with her and they also lifted his finger prints from several beer cans. Sheriff Tucker drove to the Wilson home to talk to Tyson.

As he walked to the door, he heard the back screen door slam. He ran around the house and saw Tyson running down the alley. Sheriff Tucker took after him on foot, which was a mistake. Sheriff Tucker weighed 320 pounds dripping wet. Tyson fled and was picked up in Arkansas three days later on a DWI.

Tyson was found guilty and sentenced to forty-five days before being extradited back to Indiana to face assault to face assault and battery charges. When the Arkansas Sheriff learned of Jenny Morgan's death, he told Tyson through the bars. Tyson just looked at him and lowered his head. The death of Jenny prompted the Indiana State Police to bring Tyson back for a court hearing. Tyson told a cell mate that he raped her and beat her; but didn't mean for her to die. He said that she taunted him and called him names.

When the police van pulled up to Goodland's Jail, there were several people chanting for Tyson to burn in hell. Tyson for the first time in his life was frightened. He knew he could not get out of this one.

Sheriff Tucker was right there when Tyson stepped out of the van. He was wearing wrist and leg shackles.

"I'm so glad that you have decided to stay with us, Tyson." Sheriff Tucker said with his teeth clenched. Tyson usually had a smart reply, but he looked to the ground and said nothing.

He was printed and processed and given the standard orange uniform to wear. Tyson was put in a private cell to wait for his court date. He did not receive a call or visit from his family and they would not receive his collect calls from jail. Tyson sat in his cell all alone. He thought about all the bad things that he had done as he removed the top sheet from the bed. He looped the sheet around the top bar, then around his neck and walked off the top bunk. The sheets tightened and Tyson gagged. He thought it would be a quick death, but it was not. He tried to let out a yell and tried to loosen the sheet, but was unable to free himself. Tyson stopped fighting his fate and slowly died in the cold cell by himself.

The guard that was watching the monitors of the prisoners in the jail stepped out to make a fresh pot of coffee. He stood at the coffee maker talking to another jailer about the eight point buck he had shot from a deer stand in Molters woods last Saturday.

The two jailers talked until the coffee was ready. As the jailer got back to the central control room, he looked at the monitors and sipped his coffee.

"Oh shit! Oh shit! Damn it!" He yelled as his coffee hit the floor and he hit the emergency intercom.

"All officers to cell block two, repeat, all officers to cell block two."

Two guards got there and just stared at Tyson's lifeless body hanging from the top bunk. The jailer called the paramedics and coroner. It took nine minutes for the paramedics to arrive.

"Why didn't you get him down? Open the God damn cell door!" The paramedic shouted. As the door opened, the paramedic immediately cut him down and started CPR. The color was out of his lifeless body and his pupils were fixed and dilated.

"He's dead….give me the time of death," the paramedic shouted in a frustrated voice.

"3:02p.m.," said Bob Willis, who was the county coroner.

"I called Wally and he is on his way," he said.

This saved the taxpayers a lot of money by this scum bucket hanging himself," Sheriff Tucker said with a grin.

"I'll pretend that I didn't hear that from you Sheriff." Bob said in discust.

The paramedics helped get Tyson's body into the body bag and on the coroner's cot.

"Hey Wally, you're just in time," shouted the Sheriff.

Wally walked into the cell and saw the bagged body on the steel cot.

"Wally, can you take Tyson to the county hospital for an autopsy?" Bob said.

"What the hell does he need an autopsy? That son of a bitch coward took his own life!" The sheriff exclaimed.

"This could turn into a law suit and we will do everything by the book on my watch. Clear, Sheriff?" Bob said as he glared at the sheriff.

Wally stepped in and said, "Bob's right. I'll be happy to take him to the hospital and I will bring your cot back to you when I return." Wally said as he and a jailer maneuvered the cot out of the cell.

"See you boys, my job is finished here," Bob said as he left the cell.

"Hey Bob, sorry that I got out of hand," Sheriff Tucker said.

"No problem Sheriff. I will still vote for you this November," Bob said as everyone laughed.

The jailer helped Wally guide the cot through the corridor and to the secure garage. The jailer opened the garage door so Wally could walk to his Suburban. He backed his vehicle in and loaded Tyson's body to be transported to the county hospital. Wally knew the routine. He parked his Suburban by the dumpster in back of the hospital. He had to transport the body through the kitchen and down a long hall to the general elevators in the main lobby. This elevator would take him to the basement where the morgue was. The hospital needed a better way to service the funeral directors when they bring a body to the morgue or pick a body up. This was not in the budget, nor did the administration see a need.

Wally wheeled the cot into the morgue and positioned the cot along side the stainless steel table. He carefully unzipped the body bag and saw a lifeless boy. The bruises on his neck were purple against his cold white skin. Wally walked around the table, which was the same height as the cot. He grabbed the body bag with both hands and slid it toward him on the table.

Wally started to remove the bag from around Tyson and felt a dark sensation as he touched the cold flesh. The room seemed dark and grew cold. Perspiration was running from Wally's forehead.

Wally closed his eyes and saw a big bearded man in coveralls beating a young child with a belt. The man was striking the child with the buckled end of the belt.

Wally could hear the man shout, "You stupid fucking kid, you're no son of mine…I could kill you!!"

Wally watched in horror as the man threw the boy to the ground, holding him down with his booted foot on the boy's neck. The man took a long drag from his cigarette and proceeded to burn the child's back. He screamed out in pain begging his father to stop hurting him.

"All you alright Wally?" Dr. Markus asked in a concerned voice.

Wally turned and looked at Dr. Marcus, who was the pathologist and said,

"Yea, I'm just not feeling so well. I guess I am tired from the Miller Funeral, Doc."

"That was a lovely service, Wally. Mildred and I will sure miss her. Are you sure you are alright?" He said.

Wally took a deep breath and said, "I'm sure. This is Tyson Wilson. He hung himself in the jail. It's pretty cut and dry, but the coroner's office wants an autopsy for legal reasons. We all must cover our asses. Can I pick him up tomorrow morning?" Wally said still shaken.

"No problem. Hey, get some sleep. I don't want to be performing an autopsy on you, my friend." Dr. Marcus said with authority.

Wally left the hospital very confused. He had a sick feeling in the pit of his stomach. He could not stop thinking about what he saw before Dr. Marcus entered the room.

"Was he crazy?" He thought. He felt that the Wilson boy had a lot of rage bottled up from his past and he finally blew. Wally saw the scars on his back that would explain what he saw in the basement of the hospital.

Wally drove home not knowing what he experienced or if he should tell someone. He had been a funeral director for fifteen years and nothing like this had ever happened to him. Why now? Wally decided to keep his hospital experience to himself....for now.

When Wally arrived home, there was a message from Sheriff Tucker. Wally called him and the sheriff told him that the officer delivered the news to Mrs. Wilson about the death of his son. She ordered him off of her property. She yelled for the government to dig a hole and drop Tyson in it. She was not going to pay a dime for his funeral.

Helen took a plate of food out of the oven and said, "Hon, here is what's left of your dinner."

Wally sat at the kitchen table and Helen massaged his neck and shoulders while he ate.

"If you keep rubbing me like that, I will have to carry you up to our bedroom. Wally said with a smile.

"Promises, promises. We all need to get to bed early tonight," Helen said.

"No, I promised the boys that I would take them to the movies tonight. Will you look up the Wilson number for me, hon?" Wally asked as he got up and walked over to the phone.

Wally dialed the number as Helen recited it to him.

"May I speak to Mrs. Wilson? This is Wally over at the funeral home." He said.

"Ma, it's the funeral home calling." A small child said.

Yes, this is Sue Ellen Wilson, what can I do for you, Wally?" She sharply said.

"Well, I want you to know how sorry about what happened to your son. I took him into my care and to the hospital." Wally said in a soothing voice.

"Much obliged, but I ain't claiming him. He was no good like his ole man. I ain't coming or paying. Tyson moved out and only came around when he needed something. Things came up missing after he left. That no good thieving bastard!" She said.

"I know how you must feel, your son needs a proper burial and service," Wally pleaded.

"Call the trustee. The only people to be at his funeral will be you and the grave digger. You're a nice feller Wally, but I am not doing anything for that bastard son of mine. I'll spit on his grave!" She screamed as she hung up.

Wally took the boys to the movies as promised. It was an action movie that took his mind off of his eventful day. He thought about the Miller and the Wilson Families. The only thing the two had in common was Wally.

When the county pays for a funeral, it consists of a cloth covered casket, grave liner, no service and an unmarked grave located in the paupers' section of the cemetery. No embalming is usually done. Wally did however, dress Tyson in a nice outfit that he had outgrown. Wally put Tyson in the casket and placed it in the chapel. He placed a single rose on the casket lid that was left over from the Miller service. Wally and his family stood in front of the casket and Wally said a prayer. No one came to the funeral home and no one came to the cemetery.

As they lowered the casket into the ground, Wally noticed a little girl on a bicycle. She was on the west side of the cemetery, which was higher that the place where they were burying Tyson. She stood there watching her brother's grave being covered. Wally said a grave side prayer and when he turned…she was gone.

CHAPTER 4

Wally got up early the following morning and he and Helen fixed a big breakfast for the boys.

"Let's go camping this weekend at Campland." Wally said out of the blue.

"Yea! Yea! Yea! cheered the boys.

"Wally what's the matter with you? It's freezing outside and you want to go camping! Are you crazy? Helen said with the boys cheering.

"Why you know dear…I am crazy. Besides, it will be a blast. We can build a fire, roast wieners and marshmallows, tell scary stories and snuggle in a sleeping bag. Sorry boys, you are on your own. Campland is only thirteen miles away and I will have my beeper and cell phone in case we get a call. We haven't done this in a long time… please!' Wally said.

"OK, but if I get cold or it snows, I'm coming home. You guys can stay and freeze. Got it?" Helen said.

"Can we each bring a friend, Dad? Sammy said.

"Boys, lets just do this as a family, OK? Walter asked with a smile.

The boys left for school and Helen asked Wally what possessed him to camp in this cold weather.

"Helen, when we first met, remember when we used to camp a lot? Remember how beautiful and big the sky looked at night. How cool the air was entering our lungs and sitting around a fire that would keep our feet toasty warm. We've been too busy to take the boys camping in a long while. I want to start making time for the simple things this life has to offer. Now, lets find all of our camping gear," Wally said.

Helen reached for Wally's hand and pulled him out of the chair and into her arms. She squeezed Wally and whispered, "Wally, I love you. I couldn't live without you."

Wally hugged Helen tightly and whispered, "Helen dear….I'm horny and I want you," she laughed and patted him on the butt.

Wally and Helen spent the morning gathering the tent, camp stove, sleeping bags, cooking pots and pans, and a camp heater. They packed the van, went to the grocery store and bought enough food for a week; but were only staying the weekend. Helen packed clothes and waited for the boys to get home from school.

"Wally, did something happen with the Wilson boy that you're not telling me?" she asked in a low voice.

"I really don't want to talk about it right now. Can we just forget about death for awhile and have a great time at Campland?" Wally said.

"Wally, remember how beautiful the experience was with Mrs. Miller, and the love that you felt from her. Please talk to me, Wally," she said.

Wally looked at the floor and for a second and said, "I'm a little afraid to do another funeral, to touch their hands or flesh and sense their lives. Yes, I did experience a feeling…a dark and cold feeling when I touched Tyson. It sucked the life right out of me. I felt a boy who had been beaten, lied to, unloved and blamed for everything bad that happened every minute of his life. What he did was unforgivable, but I feel that his father and all of the bad in his life led him to crime and murder. He raped and murdered a girl…a girl whose life was snuffed out at such an early age. She had hardly lived and now she is dead. Some say she was a whore and probably deserved it. How sad and pathetic to think that way. No one should die like that. I can't help but feel sorry for Tyson, too. He will never get a chance to make a wrong right. The feeling that I felt with Mrs. Miller gave me strength and an inner peace in my heart. Her life was full and she was loved. Tyson's touch chilled me to the bone. What will happen when I get the next call, Helen?" Wally said as he broke down and cried. Helen comforted him.

"I think you should have lunch with Max and tell him what happened. Max will understand," Helen said.

The boys burst into the house ready for the camping trip.

"What's wrong with dad?" asked Sammy.

"Oh, he had an eyelash in his eyes and you know what a baby your father is with pain," Helen said quickly.

"Are you ready, you little troopers?" Wally said as he chased the boys around the kitchen table.

They all loaded into the van and headed for Campland. Wally hoped that his beeper would be idle for the weekend.

"Mom, did you pack the Cheetos?" Sammy asked.

"Yes dear, I brought all the snacks that you both like." She said

"Wieners and marshmallows are all that I need! Ha. Ha. I can't wait to build the fire." Wally said with excitement!

It took twenty minutes to get to Campland. Wally filled out the registration and drove into the park.

"Dad, I like this spot, right here," Jeremy yelled.

"That does look like a nice spot. It's close to the bathrooms," Helen said.

"Us men don't need bathrooms. We've got all those trees," Wally said in a low but loud voice.

"Yea mom," Sammy agreed.

They pulled the van into the spot and Wally popped open the back hatch and said. "Let's get the tent out and set it up. The boys can gather firewood, hon. Oh, how I love it out there."

Campland was on the edge of a state forest preserve. It had big, beautiful, mature trees and many hiking paths for the novice as well as the expert hiker. The day was sunny and only one other camper was at the park on such a brisk December day.

"Wally, it is beautiful out here," Helen said as they put up the tent.

"I've missed the simple things like this. Look how happy the boys are gathering fire wood. Make sure you get some big logs, boys," Wally said smiling.

Wally had purchased a dome with a front awning that would sleep six.

"I forgot how big this tent was, Helen. When did we last use it?" Wally asked.

"I think it was five years ago or so at a church outing," Helen replied.

"Oh, yes, that's when Sammy got into that poison ivy. Hey Sammy, remember the poison ivy you got into when we went on that church camping trip? It was everywhere!" Wally said with a chuckle.

"Funny dad, you're a riot," Sammy said, rolling his eyes.

Helen and the boys unloaded the van and put all the gear inside the tent. Wally set up the lawn chairs around the fire pit. He then placed the wood carefully in the pit and started a fire. Wally stood and watched his fire burn. He looked around at the trees, the brown leaves on the ground, and the isolated beauty this place has to offer. He watched his boys and wife who he so dearly loved unload the van. They gave him such strength and love. Wally felt complete.

"You could help us you know," Helen said to Wally.

"Gosh, honey, I would like to; but I have to watch this fire. You wouldn't want it to go out would you?" Wally asked with a boyish smile.

"Thank God for your father boys. Isn't he good to us?" Helen said as she chased Wally around the fire.

The boys unrolled their sleeping bags and they all sat around the large fire. As Wally and his family sat feeling the warmth from the fire, the sun illuminated the sky with rich reds and oranges against the dark blue sky.

"What a glorious sight, if I could see heaven, it would be this sunset. I have

Never seen such a beautiful sky," Wally said as he looked at his family.

"Dad, why did you want to be a funeral director? Do you like doing it?" Sammy asked poking the fire with a stick.

"Well, your uncle Ben and I were playing in the woods behind our house. We were playing hide and go seek. I was hiding behind a stump and he found me. I got up and started running for the base with Ben right behind me. We were both laughing as he said he was going to get me. I got to the base and turned around and Ben was lying on the ground. He had slipped and hit his head on a rock. Ben was not moving, so I ran to my house. My mom called the Doctor, who rushed over. Ben was in a coma for three weeks. I came everyday after school and pleaded with him to wake up. He never did." Wally said looking at his boys.

"I remember the funeral director entering the hospital room with our family all around the bed. He asked if he could take our Ben into his care. I looked up and said, please don't take him just yet. He smiled and said for me to take all the time that I needed. Everybody left the room except me. I just looked at Ben and cried and cried.

I walked out of the room and the funeral director looked at me with the kindest eyes and said, 'Wally, your brother was a lucky little fellow to have a brother like you. God is smiling down at you and holding Ben's hand.' He made me feel at peace with the loss of my brother. I was thirteen when we lost Ben and I knew that I wanted to be a funeral director," Wally said as he and his family stared at the flames.

"Dad, I want to be just like you when I grow up," Sammy said with a smile.

"Who's ready for wieners and marshmallows?" Wally got up and shouted.

"I am, I am, I am," said the boys and Helen.

Wally handed out the coat hangers that had been converted into hot dog sticks. Helen passed out the wieners.

"I like mine burnt," Wally said as he put the hot dog directly into the flame.

"Well, you're not going to cook mine. I like mine golden brown," Helen said.

Wally and his family ate the hot dogs and roasted marshmallows and told scary stories around the fire. As the night grew colder, Wally would toss more wood onto the fire. They didn't even feel the cold. Wally went into the tent and lit the camp heater to warm up the tent.

"I have one rule boys, the first one to fart will sleep out in the van." Wally said with a serious look on his face trying to hold back the laughter.

The boys both laughed and Jeremy said, "Right Dad, it will be you sleeping in the van then."

Wally and Helen stood by the fire as the boys got into their sleeping bags.

"You were right, this is great. I don't even feel the cold and the boys are so happy," Helen said with her arms around Wally.

They held each other gazing into the fire, then entered the tent and got into their sleeping bags. It was so quiet and peaceful out there, just the sounds of winter echoing throughout the forest. They all slept like babies through the cold winter night.

The boys woke up to the smell of fresh bacon being cooked over the open fire. They got up and joined their dad by the open fire, leaving their mom to sleep.

"What time is it, Dad?" Jeremy asked, rubbing his eyes.

"7:15a.m. and we have to eat a huge breakfast before we do any exploring," Wally answered as he flipped the bacon.

"Should we wake mom?" Sammy asked.

"No, let her sleep. We will bring her breakfast in bed after we eat," Wally said.

The boys each cracked the eggs into a stainless steel bowl.

"Remember boys, no egg shells," Wally said.

They brought Helen a full plate of bacon and eggs and pancakes. The smell woke her up as they entered the tent.

"Rise and shine, my little chickadee, your breakfast is served by your slaves," Wally said.

"What time is it?" Helen asked, still half asleep.

"Why, it's a little before 8:00a.m.," Wally said.

"Let's eat and go back to sleep. I'm so comfortable," Helen said yawning.

"The boys and I have eaten. We will wait for you so that we can explore the woods," Wally said.

"You guys explore and I'll go back to sleep," Helen said as she ate a piece of crisp bacon. Helen finished her breakfast as Wally and the boys disappeared into the woods. She got up at about 10:30a.m. and enjoyed the quiet while reading a book.

"Mom, we found a dead raccoon," Sammy yelled as he entered the tent.

"Oh that sounds great; I hope you had a proper burial for him." Helen said.

"No, we wanted too, but dad didn't have a shovel. So we covered the raccoon with leaves and sticks," Sammy said.

"I'm so glad to hear that. Who wants a sandwich?" Helen asked. Wally and the boys were starved. They had gone on every trail and skipped about a thousand smooth flat stones into a pond. They sat around the fire that Helen had rekindled and had lunch.

"Dad, let's go back on the trails," Sammy said.

"Boys, knock yourselves out. You guys go and give me a report," Wally said keeping warm by the fire.

"Don't touch or bring back any dead animals," Helen said as the boys headed for the woods. Wally and Helen just sat content and happy, staring into the fire.

"Wally lets do this every weekend," Helen said with a smile.

"Boy, this is quite a change from the woman who said it would be too cold this time of the year," Wally said with a chuckle.

"I know I said that, but I never dreamed how soothing and wonderful this fire would be," Helen said as she picked up her book.

Wally cupped his hands behind his head, crossed his feet and gazed into the horizon.

"What a perfect day," He thought, "I think I'm going to take a nap. That hiking wore me out."

"I'll join you," Helen said. They entered the tent hand and hand.

The boys came out of the woods with walking sticks that they made. Sammy yelled into the tent, "Jeremy kept poking me with the stick, dad." The sound of Sammy's voice woke Wally from a calm sleep.

"Well Sammy, let's get Jeremy down and tickle him," Wally said as they chased Jeremy and gently brought him to the ground. Sammy jumped on and they started to tickle Jeremy.

"Stop, stop, stop!" Jeremy said laughing.

That night was a mirror of the night before. They enjoyed a beautiful sunset, hot dogs and marshmallows. They were all tired and slept throughout the night. The boys woke up to the bacon that their parents were preparing.

"Do we have to go home this morning? I want to stay longer," Sammy said.

"Yes, boys, we have to get back for church and wash the grime off of you both before the service. Let's eat and pack," Wally said.

"Can we bring our walking sticks home, Dad?" Sammy asked.

"Weapons we do not need at home," Wally quickly said.

"Oh, Dad!" Sammy moaned

Packing for the trip home was not as much fun as packing for the adventure. They all piled into the van and headed home. The smell of smoke lingered in their clothes, which was a fond memory of their trip to Campland.

CHAPTER 5

One by one, the boys washed the weekend off in the shower and dressed for church. Wally and his family sat in the third pew on the right side at the Presbyterian Church. The minister delivered a wonderful sermon which included a prayer for the Tyson Wilson family.

Wally thought of him little during the weekend. It got around town that no one attended the funeral, no one sent flowers, no one seemed to care; but a few nosy church members who had to gossip. Mrs. Jacobs, an eighty year old busy body was angry that Tyson was buried at the local cemetery. Wally just smiled and ignored her.

"Can you believe what Mrs. Jacobs had the nerve to say…where Tyson should have been buried? If she had it her way, he would have been fed to a pack of wild dogs," Wally said on the drive home from church.

"Wally, let's not talk about Tyson anymore," Helen said.

When they got home, Wally asked the boys if they had homework.

"Yea dad, I have some," said Jeremy.

"Me too," Sammy also said.

"You both do your homework after lunch and then you both can play," said Helen.

"I'll bet Jeremy will want to go over to Tess' and play kissy face," Sammy said in a teasing way.

"Shut up stupid," Jeremy snapped back.

"Boys settle down…and I do not want to hear that word out of your mouth again," said their mother in a stern voice.

The next morning, Wally called Max to have lunch. Max said that he was in court until 2:00p.m. and to stop by the office after that. Max is Wally's best friend. They've know each other since high school. Teresa, Max's wife is Helen's best friend. The four usually go out to dinner once a week. One of Wally and Helen's most memorable vacations was in St. Thomas with Max and Teresa. Wally knew that Max would not think he was crazy when he told him about his last two funerals.

Wally got back to Max's office in the afternoon. The secretary said that Max was still in court and to just go on back to his office.

"Would you like a cup of coffee or a soft drink?" she asked.

"No thank you Bev, I've had my caffeine for the day." Wally replied with a smile. As Max walked into the door, his secretary said that Wally was already in his office.

"Hey buddy. Sorry I had to make lunch at 2:00p.m. You know how Judge Bishop is. If he don't eat, you don't eat. What are you hungry for…my friend?" Max asked as he patted his friend on the back.

"How much time do you have? We could go to the Knickerbocker." Wally said.

"So you want to drink some beer, huh?" Max said.

"Well it did cross my mind; it's been a while since we have had early afternoon beers." Wally said with a grin.

I've got all afternoon. My four o'clock client didn't post bail. A beer and burger sounds great." Laughed Max!

"I see that you still have those high quality clients, Max," Wally said with a chuckle, as they walked to his car.

"I'll have you know my scumbag clients paid for this Mercedes," Max said as they climbed into his car.

The Knickerbockers was thirty-five minutes away. It is a great restaurant and pub with a traditional atmosphere.

"I heard that you had a tough funeral Friday…Tyson Wilson. That was the shortest life sentence I have ever seen and he didn't even go to trial. That was one murder case that I would not have taken. The public defender would have fucked it up," Max said with a coy smile.

"How is Teresa? What did you do this past weekend?" Wally asked. "Dinner and a movie…bad flick, great meal. You know how I love a great steak. The movie was one of those mushy love stories.

Hell, I can't even remember the name of it. Teresa loved it. What did you guys do?" Max asked.

"You probably won't believe it this, but we went camping at Campland," Wally said waiting for a reaction from his friend.

"Are you crazy? What possessed you to do such a thing in December?" Max asked raising his voice an octave.

"I told you that you probably would not believe it. We had a wonderful time. We had a big bonfire and the camp heater kept us warm in our tent. The quiet beauty in December was spectacular," Wally said.

"Well, the only camping Teresa would want to do is at the Hilton with room service," Max said as they pulled up to the Kickerbocker.

The restaurant was empty except for the men on barstools. They took a booth in the back.

"What can I get for you?" a red-headed waitress asked.

"I will have ice tea," Wally answered.

"Wait a minute. I didn't come here for ice tea. We both will have Old Style in a bottle," Max quickly said.

"This is just like old times, power drinking in the afternoon," Said Wally.

The waitress brought them the beers and ordered lunch.

"Max, something happened last week and I've got to tell someone. When I got to the Miller home, it happened when I was in the bedroom..."Wally said as Max interrupted.

"You didn't have sex with Mrs. Miller, did you? Max laughed.

"Oh...aren't you funny! I'm serious, listen. Before I removed her from her home, I touched her hand and I felt an erie feeling. It's like I felt her past life. I could see her childhood and I guess the meaningful things in her life. I even smelled fresh bread. The bread part must sound a little weird, don't ask, but Max, I felt a wonderful feeling from her touch. Now I probably would not have thought anything of this; but it happens with the Wilson boy as well. It was a horrible feeling and I saw horrible things...a man beating a young boy. These feelings or visions happened from the first touch while I was making the removal," Wally said.

"Let me get this straight. You had some kind of a vision, some sort of psychic power from the dead? Wally, I did read something about this," Max said with a serious look on his face.

"You did?" Wally quickly asked.

"Yes, from a publication at the checkout line at the grocery store. 'State road worker predicts future from removing road kill!" Max said laughing. They became silent when the waitress brought them their lunch.

"Have you told anybody about this? I mean, are you crazy?" Max said.

"Max, I have only told Helen. I am not making this up, I wish I were. In fact, Helen told me to talk to you about this because you are my best friend…aren't you?" Wally said in a desperate voice.

"Wally, you are my best friend. You are the kindest, most considerate person I know. I also know how much time and care you put into your funerals. I could never do what you do, nor could you do what I do; because you have a conscience. I do believe you, Wally. If this could happen to anyone, it would happen to you. I don't think I would tell anyone about this, Wally. I have had clients that I can tell are lying or are as guilty as sin. I can see it in your eyes. I have even turned down criminal cases with big payoffs because I got bad vibes from them or their families. Remember the guy who said the gun was going off when he was cleaning it and I got him off scot-free. You buried his wife," Max said.

"Yes, I remember that well. He shot her with a hollow point and I spent nine hours on her because the family did not want a closed casket." Wally said.

"That case got national attention, a story in Newsweek. Well, I got a bad feeling about this guy before I agreed to take the case. The guy had money; he even paid for our condo in Palm Springs. After the trial, when he was found not guilty, he came to my office to thank me and to settle up. He asked me if anything could change the verdict down the road. I said no that would be double jeopardy, you are a free man. He looked me straight in the eye and smiled and said… 'I shot the bitch on purpose. I guess we have a client privilege, huh?' and that prick just walked out of my office grinning from ear to ear. My job is not to judge, but to defend. Don't let what happened to you eat you up wondering why. If this continues with future calls that you deal with, this could be valuable information for the families that you serve. Now how about those Chicago Bulls." Max said as they both laughed.

"Thanks, Max, you're right. It has been eating me up wondering why. I never thought that you could sense that about your clients. I would never have thought that you would turn down a client. Maybe there is hope for you yet, my friend. Wally said with a chuckle.

"You don't need to worry about me. I sleep like a baby at night. The day my job starts bothering me, is the day that I will stop practicing law." Max said.

The two finished their meals and had a few beers. Max was probably over his legal limit, but no cop in a three county area would pull over his white Mercedes with the vanity plate that said "LAWMAN" on the license plate.

As they started for home, Wally's beeper went off. It's my answering service. I'd better call," Wally said as he reached for his cell phone.

"This is Wally at the DeVere Funeral Home. I have a message. What's the name? What nursing home? Yes, give me the number, thank-you." Wally said to the operator.

Angus Hutchens died. I've got to get home and pick him up at Hillcrest Nursing Home."

"Hey that is on the way. Let's just throw him in the trunk. It will save you a trip." Max said laughing.

"You still are a warped and sick bastard, Max…besides he wouldn't fit in your tiny trunk. Wally said with a smile.

Wally and Max talked about their next getaway with the wife's and where it might be. Max pulled into the parking lot next to Wally's Suburban and said. "Call me if the Hutchins guy says anything. I'm just kidding you my friend." Max said as he drove off.

CHAPTER 6

Wally drove home to freshen his breath and change into a coat and tie. He was greeted at the door by Helen.

"I figured that you guys would be out a little later." Helen said.

"Max has a big day tomorrow and I got a page from the service to pick up a body from Hillcrest…Mr. Hutchens. I've got to put on a coat and tie. Where are those breath mints? I don't want the family to smell alcohol on my breath." He said.

Wally backed the hearse out of the garage. Wally always used the hearse on hospital and nursing home removals. He used the Suburban on home and accident removals. Wally did not like to have the hearse in residential areas.

It is less conspicuous with the Suburban. Nursing homes are difficult because he must wheel the cot down a long corridor and everyone knows why he is there. Wally got the feeling that the residents there are just waiting for Wally to come and get them. He can see it in their sad eyes as he passes them.

Wally must check in with the front desk to handle all of the paper work. Sometimes a family is there waiting for Wally, sometimes no one.

"Could I have the paper work on Mr. Hutchens, please?" Wally said to the front desk nurse.

"We have it right here, he is in room 315. The family has already left. They wanted you to get his teeth and glasses. His sister was very concerned about that," she said with a smile.

"I'll be sure to get those things. Room 315 is down the hall, right?" Wally said.

"That's right." She said looking at her charts.

"Thank-you," Wally said as he pushed the cot down the corridor and into room 315. There was just the bathroom light on, making the room dark.

Wally turned the light on and a little old lady stopped at the doorway.

"Are you here for Angus?" She asked."

"Why yes, I am the funeral director and I am going to take him into my care," Wally said in a soft voice.

"We will sure miss him. He loved to play bridge. He was my partner on Tuesdays," she asked.

"What is your name, ma'am?" Wally asked.

"I'm Edna Taylor. I've lived in this town all my life. My grandson owns Taylor Insurance Agency on Main Street. Do you know Timmy?" She said with pride.

"Yes I do. He is a fine fellow. Thank you for sharing that with me. I will take good care of Mr. Hutchens." Wally said.

She stood there for a few seconds and then walked down the corridor to the lobby. Wally closed the door and positioned the cot next to Mr. Hutchen's bed. Wally just stood there for a moment, then placed his hand on Mr. Hutchen's forearm and closed his eyes.

Wally got a warm sensation throughout his body. He saw a shack with wooded mountains in the background. The family was sitting around an old table. They sat on two long benches made of scrap wood. The father's clothes were covered with soot as was his face. Wally could sense that he worked in the coal mines.

There were four girls and a little boy with no mamma at the table. Wally could smell soup beans and cornbread. The family was holding hands and saying grace. They prayed for Maureen, their mother, to be safe in heaven.

Wally then saw a man in uniform carrying another man to a foxhole. He could see the fear in the man's face. Wally felt goodness while watching this man.

Wally then saw a man in blue and white overalls taking a drink from a jug. Then he got on a combine to finish the field. Then he saw the man alone in a small house, sitting at the kitchen table sopping up soup beans with his cornbread. He was gazing at children playing in the yard next to him. Wally felt how lonely he was. How he should have married and had kids and how he missed his daddy after forty years.

Wally let go of his arm. The sorrow in this man's still heart was unbearable. With so much evil in the world, how could this man who's heart was pure be alone?

Wally lowered the cot even with the bed and locked the wheels. He pulled Mr. Hutchens on the cot, sliding a back board under him and then sliding the board and sheets onto the cot.

Wally positioned his hands, strapping him to the cot and carefully covering him with the body cover. Wally placed Mr. Hutchen's teeth and glasses on the cot and wheeled him out of the room and down the corridor.

As Wally headed for the door, a woman stopped him.

"Are you from the DeVere Funeral Home?" she asked.

"Why yes, I am the funeral director, Wally." He said

"Is that Angus Hutchens? He is my brother." She said

"Yes ma'am, it is." Wally said with respect.

"May I see him, please?" She said.

"Certainly you may," Wally replied as he pulled back the covers from his face.

"Where are his glasses, he always has his glasses on?" she asked.

"They are right here, ma'am. They will be safe with me," Wally said holding her hand.

"He took such good care of my sisters and me after daddy died. Angus was such a good man, always doing for others and not himself," she said as she wept.

"The only thing that made him happy was soup beans and cornbread. I know it must sound funny, but whenever he would visit my sisters or me, that's what we would fix him. It made him feel safe. Our daddy was the same way. I'm not sure why I told you that, the thought just came to me." She said.

"I will be real careful with your brother. You and your sisters call me when you are ready to come to the funeral home to make arrangements," Wally said as he handed her his business card.

"Would 8:00a.m. be too early for you?" she asked.

"No ma'am. I'll see you at 8:00am. I will be happy to help you in any way I can," Wally said as he pushed Mr. Hutchens to the hearse.

Wally drove home and realized that God had given him a heightened sense to guide him to comfort people who were touched by the angel of death.

That evening, he crawled in bed with Helen after he tucked the boys in.

"Helen, it happened again; but I feel in my own heart that God gave me this gift. I felt the presence when I touched Mr. Hutchens. I saw his life just like I did with Mrs. Miller and the Wilson boy. This time I feel as though I know how to use the gift. I have always tried to create a meaningful personal ceremony that was different from each family. I now have the tools to help families deal with the grieving process. I am going to see Mrs. Wilson and tell her that the Lord took her son to heaven." Wally said.

"You are not going to want to preach on Sundays are you?" Helen said in a concerned voice.

"No honey…Rev. Collins' job is safe, I assure you." Wally said with a grin. He kissed his wife goodnight and fell sound asleep.

At eight in the morning, three ladies came to the front door of the funeral home.

"Hello ladies…I'm Wally. I am so sorry for the loss of your brother, Angus." Wally said reassuring them. He led them into the arrangement room.

"We brought Angus' blue and white coveralls that he wore everyday until he went into the nursing home. We all decided that they would be more appropriate than a suit. No one ever saw our Angus in a suit. He always had on a clean pair of blue and white overalls." His sister said.

"We also have some pictures that we would like to be displayed. Here's our daddy with all of us in front of the home that we grew up in. I know it don't look like much…but be had such great memories there." Said another sister as the other sisters nodded their heads in agreement.

"Is that the mountains in the background? It looks like such a pretty country," said Wally.

"West Virginia, we grew up in the hills of central West Virginia about one hundred miles east of Charleston." She said with a smile.

"I took my boys white water rafting near there. That truly is God's country." Wally said.

Wally wrote down all of the important information about Angus' life. Wally smiled to himself, because he felt that he had known all of them. Before Wally took the ladies into the casket selection room, he explained all of the details and different materials that they will have to choose from. Bronze, copper, stainless steel, and the different species of wood are all possible choices.

"Before we go into that room, we have decided that we want Angus buried in an oak casket. He loved to climb the oak tree in our backyard. We had a big swing on that tree. Do you remember how Angus would push us on that swing for hours, never complaining and he refused to be pushed?" Angus' sister said as she began to weep.

"Let me give you ladies a few minutes, before I show you the oak caskets." Wally said as he left the room as the ladies told stories about their beloved brother. When Wally came back to the room, he escorted them into the casket selection room. Wally has all of the wood caskets together and they all agreed on the oak casket with an oak leaf in the cap panel of the casket.

They were very pleased with the selection and how accommodating Wally was.

The visitation was set for the following evening from five to nine p.m. and the funeral was the following morning.

Wally met with the minister, Rev Bob Collins, before the funeral. Wally felt comfortable with Rev. Bob was not only his own pastor but he was a pro at funerals. He was always early and would discuss any last minute details with Wally. Rev. Bob's energy was powerful. He always did extensive research on the lives of the deceased, especially if he did not know the person or the family.

Rev. Bob had a funeral for a retired judge who was a miserable individual. The judge would take advantage of the legal system to benefit himself.

His daughter's wedding day, which fell on a Sunday the judge called the owner of the local liquor store and asked him if he could deliver some cases of champagne fine wines and cordials. The judge had a powerful influence and convinced the store owner to deliver the spirits to him on a Sunday which prohibits the sale of alcohol. The liquor store owner obligated and sent the judge the bill for several hundred dollars for the delivery.

Several weeks later, the store owner called the judge to see if he received his bill for the champagne, fine wines and cordials. The judge snapped back at him on the phone and said;

"You delivered liquor to me on a Sunday! Selling liquor on Sunday is against our laws so I assumed that it was a gift. I will not pay a dime for it. Do you understand?" The judge shouted.

The store owner was shocked that the judge would not pay when he had been so accommodating. He feared the judge as did many other people, and did not pursue the payment of the bill.

This judge had a heart of coal. When he died, the family called Rev. Bob to conduct the funeral. Rev. Bob talked to so-called friends and family and could not find one good memory of the judge. At dinner the night before the funeral, Rev. Bob mentioned to his wife and family that no one said anything nice about the judge. Rev. Bob's son spoke up and said the judge let him ride on his golf cart last summer when he was walking. The judge was nice to him. Rev. Bob built the eulogy around the experience of his own son and delivered a beautiful funeral sermon. The judge's family was very happy.

Wally thought if anyone would understand his situation, Rev. Bob would. Rev. Bob was very active in the community. He was also a state police chaplain. He would always be called if there were a fatality. He would then give the news to the family of the victims. He was kind and giving. Rev. Bob got along with everyone. He could cut up and be funny; but on Sundays, he owned the pulpit. His sermons were magnificent. One would have to be pretty tired or hung over to nap when he commanded the pulpit.

Bob was a friend to Wally.

"Bob, I would like to give you a little more information about Angus Hutchins," Wally said.

"Sure Wally, I've already talked to his sisters and Joe Dawson, Angus' employer for over thirty years. Any more information would also be helpful, my friend." Rev. Bob said with a smile.

"Well, actually this information is from Angus," Wally said in a shaken voice.

"Did you talk to him before he died?" Rev. Bob asked.

"Well not exactly, it's a long story. How about lunch at Denny's Diner?" Wally asked.

"Sure Wally, you know I will never turn down a free lunch, especially at a place that has the best butterscotch pie in the county." Rev. Bob said with a smile.

When they got to the diner, they ordered. Wally began to tell the pastor about Mrs. Miller, the Wilson boy and Angus Hutchens. Rev. Bob gave Wally all of his attention. He was such a good listener. Wally was in tears as he passionately told about his experience.

"Do you think I need professional help, Bob?" Wally asked as he wiped the tears out of his eyes.

"Wally, I have enjoyed working with you on funerals. When I receive a call about a death, I am relieved when it's your funeral home that the family has chosen. You make my job so easy, because we work so well together, like teamwork. You are the most organized, caring and all around the best funeral director that I have ever worked with in my thirty five years in the ministry. Wally, you do not need professional help, nor are you crazy. I can't explain what you are feeling, but it is a wonderful gift. When you told me about the Wilson boy, I always felt that he was a good boy inside; but his life of growing up had hardened him and made him mean. He once came to me and said he wanted to kill himself. He told me stories about his dad beating him over and over. He also told me that his uncle would get drunk and rape him as a young child. Tyson never had a chance. I, like you, believe that there is a place in God's kingdom for the Tyson's of the world. Wally, be who you are and never lose the drive and your love for the funeral business." Rev. Bob said as he patted Wally on the hand.

"Thank you, Bob," Wally said.

That Sunday, Rev. Bob delivered a message about the power of touch. Wally and Helen just looked at each other and smiled.

Chapter 7

The following week was uneventful. Wally got caught up on some paper work, while Helen painted the kitchen. She brought Wally some curtain samples to choose from for the kitchen windows. Wally said, "Whatever makes you happy…you choose." Wally said with a non- caring smile.

"I'm so glad that we are going out with Max and Teresa this evening. It seems like forever since we last went out." Helen said.

"Did you and Teresa decide on a restaurant?" Wally asked.

"Teresa heard about an Italian restaurant on Wells Street in the city. She told me that Max wants to drive because he feels like he is in a funeral procession in our black Cadillac. Did you see the new Jag that he bought Teresa for her birthday?" I want one." Helen said.

"If I were an attorney, we could drive cars like that. You know that families that we serve would not appreciate that. I got grief at Rotary when I pulled up to the meeting in a new Suburban. I do not think a Jag makes Teresa any happier… do you?" Wally said

"Maybe not, but her diamonds probably do." Helen said with a laugh.

The boys walked into the kitchen after school and yelled, "Mom, were home and hungry!"

"Boys, you do not have to yell. I'm down here." Helen said from behind the table painting trim.

"What's for dinner?" Jeremy asked.

"Your father and I are going out to dinner with Max and Teresa. You guys can pick out a video and we will order you a pizza." Helen replied.

"Can I have a friend over, mom?" Jeremy asked.

"Me too, me too, mom!" Sammy interrupted.

"You both can have one friend over. No R rated movies or scary ones. You know how Sammy is. We are leaving at 5:30p.m.," Helen said.

"I'm going to call Pete," Jeremy exclaimed.

"Mom can I call Ben?" We won't break anything, I promise," Sammy pleaded.

"Boys, just for your information, I have rigged up a series of cameras outside to watch your every move. No parties or girls over at that house while we are gone. I will have a monitor with me at all times," Wally said sternly.

"Yea, right Dad…like where is your monitor?" asked Jeremy.

"I didn't know that Dad had hidden cameras in the house." Sammy said confused. Wally, Helen and Jeremy burst out laughing.

"You're all so funny," Sammy replied stomping out of the room. Helen started to get ready as Wally put on his Khakis, jean shirt and hounds tooth three button sport coat. He sat in front of the TV flipping through the channels. Wally knew that if he tried to hurry Helen, she would go that much slower, so he just surfs the channels and waits for Helen to get ready.

Max pulled up at 5:30p.m. sharp. Max is never late, unless he is in court; which is out of his control. Teresa was already in the back seat when Wally and Helen kissed the boys goodbye. They both came out the backdoor. Wally sat in the front seat and Helen sat in the back with her best friend.

"Oh my gosh, this car is beautiful. Don't you just love it?" Helen asked.

"You know that Max bought this for me on my birthday last week, but I have yet to drive it." Teresa said.

"I am just breaking the car in, besides I would like to drive the car before it gets banged up." Max said with a laugh.

"Do you know a good divorce lawyer, dear?" Teresa asked Helen.

"Teresa, I could take Max to the crematory and it would be a whole lot cheaper way to get rid of him. Wally said with a wink.

"With friends like you, who needs enemy's," Max fired back.

"It's so good to see you guys again." Teresa said with a smile.

"Well, we could do this more often if Wally's phone would stop ringing on the weekends." Max said.

"From now on I am going to run an ad in the local paper…. please die on a Monday or Tuesday." Wally said with a laugh.

The four talked all the way to Chicago and a valet parked the car in front of the restaurant. They all went into the lounge and waited for their 7:00p.m. reservation.

"This place is very nice," said Helen.

"Now I know why Max drove, so I could pick up the check," laughed Wally.

"No, no, my friend… this evening is on Teresa and myself. I settled quite a large estate and we could not think of two people that we would like to be and celebrate with than you both. My client thought that she was entitled to her third husband's estate. The man's biological son did not. He was wrong, which meant a big payday for me," Laughed Max.

"How can you live with him Teresa?" asked Wally.

"Well we have to have a big enough house to fit his head through the door." Teresa replied with a smile.

"Yeah, all 7500 square feet of it," Max said as the hostess came to serve them. After they were seated, Max ordered the wine that Teresa was fond of.

"So Wally, I want to hear about your experience with your last three funerals. Max told me and I didn't tell a soul. I hope you are not mad," Teresa said with concern.

"Oh, I'm not mad. It's just that it is a little strange to talk about. I don't want to end up on some talk show or on the front page of the National Enquirer." Wally said.

"I think it is beautiful, the way Max described it. I have gotten feelings of vibes from people, some good and some bad. Max, remember that taxi driver in New York last year when we were at the Law Conference?" Teresa asked.

"Yes, you mean Charles Manson with a turban," Max said with a roll of his eye.

"Yes, yes, this guy gave me the creeps. We had to ride about sixteen blocks to get to the theatre. I made him stop after three blocks. He looked as though he had just killed someone," Teresa laughed.

"Teresa, what I experienced with Mrs. Miller and Mr. Hutchens was their past life before my eyes in only a moment. I felt as though I had known both of them quite well all of their lives. The images and colors that I saw were so real. I could even smell and taste the moment," Wally said.

"What did you smell?" asked Teresa.

"This may sound odd, but fresh bread and soup beans and cornbread," Wally said.

"Maybe you were hungry at the time," Teresa said.

"No, these were foods that they were fond of. When they found the Morgan girl, I wanted to string Tyson up, as did the whole town. I am not saying what he did was not brutal, but I felt sorry for his life that led him to crime. Maybe I will experience this with the next body or never again. I think it has made me a better funeral director." Wally said with a smile.

"You are already a great funeral director Wally," Teresa said.

"He was waiting for someone to say that. He's as bad as Max. Teresa, why do men need to feel superior?" asked Helen.

"Because they have woman like us dear," Teresa said with a chuckle.

"We have a surprise for you. I got tickets to the Comedy Shack on Rush Street," said Max.

"But why do we need to see comedians when Helen and Teresa have us?" laughed Wally.

"When Max got the bill, he looked at his wife and said, do you know that the wine was $375.00 a bottle? You sure know how to pick it!" Max said reaching for his credit card.

Teresa looked at Max and said, "Only the best, babe." Helen agreed.

Max paid the bill and gave the ticket to the valet and they waited for their car. When they arrived at the Comedy Shack, Max gave the door man the tickets that said VIP on them. They were taken to a table on the front row.

"How did you manage this, Max, the front row table?" asked Wally.

"I got these tickets from a client who was out of town tonight and he didn't want them to go to waste. What happens on the front row?" asked Max.

"Well, the people usually get heckled by the comedians. We are sitting targets, a funeral director and an attorney," laughed Wally.

"Well, then I suggest you don't tell them your profession," Max said as they ordered drinks before the show.

They all laughed so hard at the talent. It seemed as if all the comedians made fun of everyone in front except those at their table. One couple was so humiliated that they walked out.

The last act was a tall skinny man with red orange hair. His routine was great until he said seven words that stopped the laughing at their table.

"Is there an attorney in the house?"

They all looked at Max and Wally said, "Don't say a word.

"Right here!" roared Max.

"Does any one have a gun? It looks as though you haven't missed a meal, business bust be good." The comedian said in a soft but firm voice.

The crowd roared with laughter. Max stood up.

"Those are old jokes, boy, why don't you get some clothes that fit…goodwill boy. Does your hair glow in the dark…stop sign head," Max was so loud and had such a quick wit, that the comedian left him alone and picked another victim.

"Hey buddy; if your law practice doesn't work out, there is room for you at the mike." The comedian said before he closed the show.

They all laughed about Max's new found talent in life. After the show they got into the car for the trip home.

"You have no idea what it is like to live with him," Teresa said.

"I'm going to practice my routine on Judge Bishop," Max said as he pulled into Wally and Helen's drive.

"We had such a great time. Thank-you guys," said Helen.

"Our pleasure, let's go out next weekend, OK?" Teresa said.

"See you…buddy," Wally said as they drove off.

They walked into the back door of the residence part of the funeral home and into the living room. The boys were all camped out on the floor in front of the TV watching a movie. Sammy and his friends were sound asleep.

"Did you boys have fun tonight?" Wally asked.

"The girls just left before you guys got here and they took the beer with them," Jeremy said with a smile.

"It would not shock me, son." Wally said shaking his head.

"Can we stay up and finish our movie?" asked Jeremy.

"Sure, but don't stay up all night." Helen replied.

Wally picked up Sammy and Helen picked up his friend. They carried them to Sammy's bedroom and tucked them into bed. Wally and Helen walked into their bedroom, changed into their pajamas and hopped into bed. Wally turned on the TV with the remote.

"Wasn't that fun, Wally? Do you think Max had that all planned, you know how he is?" Helen asked.

"No, the comedian was truly upset that someone got the best of him while he was on stage." Wally said as he flipped through the channels. They watched TV for about an hour to unwind and went to sleep.

The next morning, Sammy and his little friend knocked on the door.

"Mom…we are hungry!" Sammy said.

"Go make some toast, boys," Wally yelled.

"But we want a big breakfast…please dad," pleaded Sammy.

Helen yawned and said. "Make the boys biscuits and gravy, hon."

"Give me ten minutes, boys. You don't even like biscuits and gravy. I guess that means that you are going back to sleep," Wally told Helen as he got up.

"Wake me up for lunch," Helen said as she rolled over.

By the time Wally got to the kitchen, all four boys were up and ready to eat. "We're going to have a man's breakfast, not a sissy breakfast. Who wants biscuits and gravy? Wally bellowed.

The boys shouted, "I do, I do!"

Wally had to make two big skillets full to feed the four hungry boys. After breakfast, Jeremy and Sammy's friends went home.

CHAPTER 8

After Church on Sunday, Wally took the family to a local restaurant that had a great brunch. The boys always liked a big meal and Helen was happy not to have to cook it. In the middle of the meal, Wally's beeper went off and Wally looked at the number.

"It's my answering service. I'm going to use the pay phone; I left my cell phone out in the car." Wally said.

As Wally walked to the phone, he was stopped by a person who told him what a nice funeral he had for Mrs. Miller. He asked Wally about his family. Wally talked for a minute or two and then he excused himself and made his call. He walked back to the table with a saddened look.

"What's wrong, Wally?" Helen asked with concern in her voice.

"Paul and Mindy's boy, Justin, drowned in the bathtub." Wally said shaking his head.

"Oh my God, how horrible…let's go boys, Daddy has to get home." Helen replied.

The boys stuffed their mouths before getting up from the table. They all got into the van and headed for home.

"I have to pick him up at the hospital. The paramedics did all they could and took him to the County Hospital. He was DOA," Wally said as he drove off. The ride to the hospital seemed to take forever. This was one trip that Wally was not looking forward to. The death of a child is indescribable. It is the most difficult funeral for a funeral director to have. No matter how seasoned you are as a funeral director, emotions flow and no one knows why a child is taken from this world…but they all feel the bitter pain from the loss.

Justin Thompson was three years old. He had snow white hair with a tint of blond and beautiful pale blue eyes. Justin could entertain people for hours with his animated charm. He would show off to anybody that was watching. He had an older brother who was twelve and a sister, seventeen. The Thompson's have a very nice Dutch Colonial two story house just three blocks from the funeral home.

Wally remembered last summer, Justin riding on his big wheel on the sidewalk. Justin's brother, Jimmy was always sick. He suffered from asthma and would get several attacks that almost took his life. He would play for hours with Justin. Oh, how he loved and protected his younger brother.

His sister, Kate, was very popular and in about every school activity. She was runner-up on the homecoming court. She was exceptional student and her parents were very proud of her.

Paul Thompson is an engineer at an auto manufacturing facility, thirty miles south of Goodland. He was chief design in the research and development area of the plant.

Mindy Thompson teaches English at the High School. She is also the track coach. Justin loved to be at his mom's track meets. He was the team mascot because he was so cute and cuddly.

Kate had started to run bath water and left the bathroom to get shampoo. She closed the door, but it cam ajar and Justin walked in and put his toy boat in the water. As he reached for the boat, he fell into the water face down. Justin couldn't turn over. He gasped in panic and filled his lungs with water. He was face down when Kate came into the bathroom. Her screams brought everyone running.

Paul ran in and swept Justin in his arms and told Mindy to call 911. He attempted CPR, but was not sure how to do it on a small child. In minutes, the paramedics arrived and rushed Justin to the hospital. They desperately tried to revive Justin, but it was too late. His precious little life was ended by a tragic accident for which no one could be blamed.

Wally got to the hospital and took his cot out of the Suburban. He had a special child body cover that was used in cases like this. Wally was glad that it was seldom used. He walked into the emergency room and left the cot behind at the nurse's station. The fact that Wally knew the family was very hard on him. The Thompson's were in the emergency room with Justin. There were huddled around his little body, not wanting to let go of his life.

Wally just stood back waiting for the Thompson's if they needed him. Mindy had Justin cradled in her arms, singing his favorite lullaby by James Taylor;

'Well, the sun is surely sinking down,
And the moon is surely rising,
and this ole world is surely spinning round,
and I do love you.
So close your eyes, you can close your eyes
It's alright
I don't know no love songs,
And I can't sing the blues anymore
But I can sing this song
And you can have this song when I'm gone.
It won't be long before another day.
We're going to have a good time.
No ones going to take our time away.
You can stay as long as you like.
So close your eyes,
You can close your eyes, it's alright
I don't know no love songs.
And I can't sing the blues anymore.
But you shall have this song when I'm gone.

Paul walked over to Wally, his face was red and his eyes were wet from tears.

"I'm so terribly sorry about Justin, Paul." Wally said.

"My boy is gone Wally, my boy's gone." Paul said as he hugged Wally in tears.

"I'm so sorry Paul." Wally said over and over again. Paul tried to get back his composure.

"What are we going to do now, Wally? Paul said confused.

"Paul, you and Mindy take your time with Justin and then I will take him into my care." Wally said stepping back.

Many of their relatives and friends had arrived in the waiting room. Kate and Jimmy left the emergency room. Jimmy had to hold Kate up. She was crying…numb with the sharp pain of their loss. Paul and Mindy knelt down right next to their little boy. Mindy kept stroking his precious face with the back of her hand. Paul held his little hand. Wally stood back and let them have all the time that they needed.

A nurse came in and told Wally that they needed the room and they would have to vacate soon. Wally ushered her out of the room and told her that they will take all of the time that they needed. "The hospital can use the other two emergency rooms." Wally walked back into the room.

"Do we have to leave now, Wally?" Mindy asked sobbing.

"No, take all the time you need with Justin." Wally said.

After some time, Paul and Mindy got up and embraced each other tightly, weeping with broken hearts.

"Wally, will you be gentle with our Justin?" Mindy asked, having trouble catching her breath.

Wally walked up to both of them and put each arm around the couple and said a prayer.

> *"Dear heavenly father, please look after these*
> *fine people in their hour of need. Give them strength*
> *to cope with their loss. Take Justin into your arms*
> *and hold him tight in your kingdom. Amen."*

Wally gently patted the couple on their shoulders.

"Thank-you Wally, Take care of my boy, Wally," Mindy said as they walked out of the emergency room arm in arm and glancing back.

Wally walked up to Justin. He looked down at this sweet prince, lying peacefully as if in a deep sleep. Wally began to cry and thought of his own boys and how much he loved them. He reached down and held Justin's tiny hand. Wally dropped to his knees and closed his eyes.

The room became bright and Wally could feel the warmth on his face like August sunshine at midday.

As the tears stopped running down his face, Wally couldn't help but smile. Circling Justin were angels dressed in all of the colors of the rainbows…bright greens, yellows, blues, violets, reds…more colors than Wally had ever seen. They all seemed to have their eyes on Wally. In the center of the angels was a child being gently held, with eyes as blue as the Pacific Ocean and beautiful blond hair. This child left Wally's heart filled with pure joy.

An orchestra of music filled the room, soft strings and soothing horns were playing. This music was the most Wally had ever heard. Wally saw a field of golden wheat behind the angels swaying back and forth from a soft breeze. The field seemed to be unending.

"Justin, can you hear me?" Wally asked with a smile.

The child looked at Wally and smiled.

"I am going on a journey to paradise where there is no pain or sorrow. You saw me here with my brother and sister, Wally. I am so loved here."

"What do I tell your parents and family?" Wally asked.

"You already know what to tell them and they already know that I am on a journey to the heavens. Wally, you are only a messenger to help people understand and cope with life beyond death," the boy said as he and the other angels faded into the wheat field. Wally just watched the wheat sway in the gentle wind with the clear blue sky in the background.

Wally opened his eyes to see the small child lying on the sheet in the emergency room. Wally looked around the room and felt a true peace, knowing that Justin left this world to be in a better place. Wally left the room to get his cot and wheeled it into the emergency room. He gently picked up Justin and held him in his arms before he placed him on the cot.

Wally covered him and wheeled him through the back doors to his Suburban. As Wally drove home, he could still hear the sweet voice communicating with him as he held Justin's hand. Wally still felt sad for the Thompsons. He knew there would be a long road in dealing with the loss of their beloved son. Wally also thought about the guilt Kate must feel by leaving the water in the tub. This will probably haunt her for the rest of her life, but Wally knew if she felt the warmth from Justin as did he, she would be at peace. Wally also knew that her little brother is now cradled in his Grandmother's arms…the Grandmother who passed away several years ago. Wally backed the Suburban into the garage, closed the door and just sat there.

"I thought I heard you pull in, dear." Helen said.

"I've been here for about fifteen minutes," Wally said with a forced smile.

"The boys are at my mother's are you OK?" Helen asked putting her arms around Wally.

"This was the hardest removal that I have ever gone on since I have been a funeral director. Remember the Jones girl who was hit by a car. I did not know the family and now I know that I did not give them the comfort that they needed." Wally said as his eyes welled up with tears.

"Wally, don't do that to yourself. You are so good with the families. You always have been." She said.

"Helen, I saw angels dressed in all the colors of the rainbow with the softest, kindest eyes that I have ever seen. It was crystal clear picture. I feel so bad for the Thompson's, but I saw Justin at peace and so loved by these angels. I felt that these angels were all family members and you know that makes perfect sense. We started on this earth with Adam and Eve. Then after centuries of multiplying, we have different races, nationalities and different personalities. What I think I saw today when I held Justin's little hand was a melting pot of love between all who enter the kingdom of heaven. Helen. I know that Justin is safe and loved, but the Thompson's will feel empty until their deaths. I am so tired." Wally said.

"Wally, I love you so much that it hurts." Helen said.

Wally's phone was ringing off the hook with people wanting to know about Justin and the times of visitation and the funeral. Wally purchased a large fruit basket and took it to the Thompson's home. He was greeted by Mindy's mother at the door, her face puffy from crying. She asked Wally to come in.

"I brought your family this basket. I thought the kids would like a healthy snack." Wally said.

"Thank-you…I'm sure we will all enjoy the basket. Paul is in the study and Kate and Mindy are upstairs in Mindy's bedroom. Jimmy is with his grandfather, just riding around the countryside. Jimmy loves to do that with his grandfather. Let me get Paul for you," she said.

Paul stepped out of his office and welcomed Wally.

"I did not mean to disturb you Paul, but I would like to speak with you." Wally said.

"Come in and sit down. I know that we have to make arrangements at your funeral home, Wally. Mindy is dreading that." Paul said as he began to weep.

"Paul, we can do that here in your home if you wish." Wally said.

"You would do that? Oh I think it would be easier for us all." Paul said wiping his eyes.

"Would you like for me to come at about seven this evening? I will bring information with me for you to make your choices in the comfort of your home. Paul, I have been a funeral director for fifteen years. I have seen different things through the years…lots of lives lost. Your son is at peace without pain or sorrow. I'm sure of that. Again, I am sorry to take up your time." Wally said grasping for words.

Paul looked at Wally and said, "Thank-you, I needed to hear that.

Wally smiled and walked out and went home.

Wally made several phone calls and got Justin's date of birth and other information from the Thompson's minister. As much information as he could get to lessen the burden to the Thompson's. Wally sat in his office and Helen brought him some hot chocolate.

"I thought this would be good for your heart, you sweetie pie. I even went to the store and got some mini marshmallows that you like." Helen said as she handed Wally the cup.

"Thank-you, Hon. I am going to the Thompson's at seven to make all of the arrangements. I know that Mindy will be in no shape to come here. I am going to suggest they have the funeral on Wednesday instead of Tuesday, to give them one more day to prepare. This in one time that I hope that I don't get death calls until this funeral is over." Wally said taking a sip.

Wally left the house at 6:45p.m. for the Thompson's home. He rang the doorbell and was greeted by Paul. Wally knew that they were in no shape to make rational decisions, everything would be a blur. He knew he had to really direct this arrangement.

"Wally, can we do this at the kitchen table?" Paul asked.

"Absolutely, Paul, that will be perfect," Wally said as he walked to the kitchen table.

"Kate did not want to come down. She is so upset, Wally. I will get Mindy." Paul said.

"Paul, would you mind if I talked to Kate please?" Wally said.

"Sure, she is up in her room; but she will probably not want to talk to you. I'll take you up there, Wally." They went up to Kate's room and Paul knocked.

"Who is it?" Kate asked.

"Kate, dear, it's Wally. He would like to speak to you," Paul said.

"Dad, I'm such a mess. I really don't want to see anyone," she said.

"Kate, I've seen messes…when my boys come in from playing outside. May I please speak with you?" Wally asked.

"Ok, you can come in," Kate said as she sat up on the bed and crossed her legs. She had a heart shaped pillow held to her chest with both arms.

"Paul will you excuse us please?" Wally asked.

"Sure, I will be downstairs." Paul said with a smile closing the door behind him.

Wally sat on Kate's desk chair and looked at a girl who had a heavy burden on her heart. The weight was unbearable. Wally could see it in her red eyes.

"Kate, may I tell you a story? All you have to do is listen…OK." Wally said handing her a box of tissue and her nodding.

"There was a boy who loved his big brother so much. He worshipped the ground he walked on. At times he would be hurt when his brother didn't want to include him because he was too little, but he was there when his younger brother needed him. One day they were playing "hide and go seek" and the younger brother was hiding. As the big brother found him, the younger brother got up and ran for base so he didn't have to be it. As he got to the base, he looked back and his brother was not behind him. He had slipped and hit his head on a rock. The little boy had lost his only brother, his best friend. He felt he was to blame and could not forgive himself.

If only he had let his big brother tag him. Kate, you did nothing wrong. I'm the little brother. You see, I lost my brother and I couldn't understand why God would let this happen. At the funeral, the funeral director told me that my brother was in the kingdom of heaven with no pain or sorrow just an abundance of love and joy. Kate, we will never be able to bring Justin or my brother back. They are in heaven, probably playing "hide and go seek" together. When I took you brother into my care, I felt that he was smiling down at me and your family. It's ok to grieve, it's ok to cry. You will miss him as will your family. There is not a day that goes by that I do not think of my brother. Kate, Justin is safe."

Kate hugged him as her tears rolled down her face and Wally comforted her.

"Thank-you Wally." Kate said in a whisper.

"I'm going downstairs to help your family plan for your brother's celebration of his life. You can come down if you like Kate." Wally said as he closed her door.

Wally met Paul and Mindy in the Kitchen. Jimmy was still with his grandparents. Wally helped the Thompson's with the arrangements and soon Kate joined them. They all stopped talking and she was embraced by her mother and father. Wally had made a difficult time in a parent's life a little easier.

The day of the visitation, the flowers kept coming, almost until the funeral service the next day. The visitation was huge; many people that didn't even know the Thompson's came to pay their respects to the family. The funeral was well attended as well. The pews in the church were full. People were also lined up on the sides and the back of the church. Wally was relieved to get this funeral behind him. He felt that the Thompson's hearts were so heavy with the loss of their son. It would take a lot of time to heal.

Wally spent the rest of the day after the funeral delivering flowers to the nursing home, churches and hospitals. The Thompson's were happy that someone could enjoy the beauty of the fresh flowers.

That evening, Wally sat in his chair watching a ball game with his boys. He couldn't take his eyes off of them lying on the floor in front of him. Sammy was swinging his little leg as he lay on his belly. Jeremy lay sideways on a pillow. Wally was so thankful to have his family and how blessed they were. Wally dozed off and was awakened by Helen.

Let's go to bed, honey." She said.

"Where are the boys?" Wally asked still half asleep.

"They boys have already gone to bed. Come on, it's been a long week." Helen said as they climbed the stairs.

"I want to just look at them sleep…OK." Wally said turning down the hall to the boy's bedroom.

"You are such a nut, and that's why I love you." Helen said as they opened the door and watched the two boys peacefully sleep.

Chapter 9

The following morning, Wally had a big breakfast with the boys and started catching up on some paperwork and paying bills.

"Wally, let's see an afternoon movie. I'll get the paper to see what's playing. We could be back before the boys get home from school." Helen said.

No hon. I've got so much to do," Wally said.

"It can wait. Let's go right now. You can do your paperwork tomorrow," pleaded Helen.

Wally thought for a moment and said, "I guess your right, but I get to pick the movie. He got up to go to the shower and change. As Wally was in the shower, the phone rang.

"Who called sweetheart?" Wally asked as he dried off.

"Bob Willis. He wants you to call him." Helen said.

Wally got dressed and dialed the phone.

"Hello Bob, its Wally."

"Thanks for calling me back. I've got a strange one. The State Police found a body that appears to have been thrown out of the car. He had no ID, no tattoos or scars. They ran prints and found nothing. He was found on Highway 41 thirteen miles north of Goodland. He will be taken down to St. Augustine Hospital. They have a crime pathologist coming from Indianapolis. If he can't be identified, you will have to pick him. Oh, I forgot an important fact. They found a 22 slug in the back of his head, which is the most common slug there is. This is exciting. We have never had a homicide like this one in our county. I have to go. Channel five wants to interview me…see ya, Wally." Bob said.

"Honey, are you ready?" Wally asked.

"Let's get a paper on the way," Helen said as they got into the suburban.

"The State Police found a John Doe north of town," Wally said as he backed the Suburban out of the driveway.

"The guy was shot, and they found no identification when they ran his prints. If the guy has no prints on file, he must not be a criminal. This guy is someone's son or brother. Gosh, Helen he could be…"

Helen Interrupted, "Let's change the subject. If you were a garbage collector, would you talk about garbage all the time? No. Let's not talk about death for the rest of the day…OK." Helen said reaching for his arm.

"OK, but if I get to pick out the movie," Wally said.

"Deal, OK…hear me out. On the last four funerals, I touched the body and felt something each time. What if I go to St. Augustine and touch this John Doe? Maybe I could be of some help. What if I disappeared, wouldn't you want to know what happened to me? This guy could be a loving husband and father." Wally said.

"You knew of the last four people that you provided a service for. This is a little different. If you want to make a fool out of yourself, go for it. Now, no more talking about death. I want to get mentally prepared for a love story that we are going to see." Helen said with a smile as Wally rolled his eyes.

Wally thought about this all through the movie and on the way home. He knew he would have an experience like the others when he touched the body.

Wally phoned Bob Willis, the coroner, the following day.

"Hello Bob, its Wally. I was wondering if you are going to St. Augustine?"

"As a mater of fact, I am going down tomorrow. They are going some DNA tests before he is released. Do you want to ride down with me?" Bob asked.

"Sure, if you don't mind." Wally said.

"Hell no, I could use the company. I'll pick you up at 8:15 a.m." Bob said.

Wally thought about this all evening. He was not going to give out any information unless he felt it was factual. What if he solved a missing person case? Wally felt that the family of John Doe deserved to know, especially if he was a devoted father.

"Honey, is something on your mind? You have been preoccupied all day." Helen questioned.

"No dear…well… I have been thinking about John Doe." Wally said waiting for Helens reaction

"Wally, do not get involved, promise me, this is crazy." Helen said shaking the brush at Wally.

"Sweetie Pie, I am already involved. We have a dead body and I'm the funeral director. Don't worry your pretty little head. Now come here and give me a kiss!" Wally said.

Bob picked Wally up at 8:15 a.m. and they stopped for coffee and breakfast to go on the way.

"I think the DNA nonsense is ridiculous. This guy has been printed and his picture faxed for identification. He is probably some schmuck that had his 'pee-pee' out and a jealous husband popped him in the head. This guy is clean-cut and shaven, nice clothes on his back. Five days in the morgue and he is all yours, Wally. Damn, I should have been a detective," Bob said as he took a bite of his apple fritter.

They arrived at St. Vincent Hospital and went down to the morgue in the basement.

"We are early. I said 9:00 a.m. and no one is here yet. They walked into the waiting area, just outside of the morgue. A page sounded over the intercom for Bob Willis. Bob walked to the nurse's station in a brisk walk to use the phone.

"This is Bob Willis; I have a message, please." Bob said out of breath.

"Why yes Mr. Willis, the message is from the State Police. The gentleman that was supposed to meet you here had to cancel. He rescheduled your meeting for tomorrow, same time," The nurse said as Bob thanked her and hung up.

"Shit, I've got to come back here tomorrow. Don't these guys know that I'm not full time and I have better things to do with my time than run down here at their beck and call?" Bob said to Wally.

"Bob, I am going to examine the body. I just want to see what I will have to work with," Wally said.

"Aren't you going to cremate the body? Bob asked.

"No…they might want to exhume the body, besides the trustee will pay for a cloth covered casket. I want to give this John Doe a proper burial," said Wally.

"You go right ahead. I have some paperwork to do up here. He is in the refrigerator unit on the south end of the room. You will find him in F-1." Bob said walking off.

Wally took the stairs to the basement and walked into the morgue. If you ever wanted peace and quiet in a hospital, visit the morgue. It's not a place many want to go to spend their time. Wally was glad that no one was around. He went to the refrigerated unit and opened the stainless steel insulated door. He pulled the sliding tray out to expose the body. The toe was tagged John Doe.

The body had already had an autopsy and the chest cavity was sewn closed. John Doe had not started to decompose and must have been found shortly after he was shot and killed.

Wally noticed that the body had been washed, but the ink on the fingertips was still visible. John Doe was in the mid to late forties, clean shaven, short hair and fingernails bitten to the quick. He must have been a nervous or hyper-individual. Wally quickly noticed that his hands were not callused. They showed the presence of little or no manual or physical labor.

He had the appearance of an all-American male…but who is this John Doe?

Wally thought carefully and looked at the door to make sure that no one was coming in or looking at him. He drew a deep breath as he closed his eyes and placed his hand on the forearm of the lifeless body. As Wally squeezed the forearm, he buckled at the knees and became as cold as ice. Perspiration poured from his face and his chest tightened.

Wally saw a young boy walking a dog down as alley on a leash. As the boy approached a low hanging wire that spanned from the building to building, he looked around to see if anyone was in the alley. He picked up the small dog with one hand, holding the leash tightly with the other. Then he tossed the dog over the wire.

The boy held the leash with both hands, watching the dog struggle to escape, kicking his paws. The boy just stood there and smiled as the dog slowed down its movement and stopped. The boy looked at the dog and poked at its face to see if any life was left in the animal. He then let the dog down from the ground, unhooked the leash, put it in his pocket and calmly walked out of the alley whistling a tune. At that moment, Wally tried to open his eyes and release his hold on the corpse, but he could not.

Wally then saw a man following a woman in a nice older neighborhood of a large city. The man stayed at a distance as he followed her. The woman wore a sleeveless dress, so it appeared to be summertime. It was also a dark night, except for the street lights that illuminated the street. She showed no sign of fear, so she must not have known that the man was following her. Wally noticed something in the man's right hand, but he could not make it out. The woman turned into an alley and the man looked around and ran to the end of the alley behind her.

Just before he reached the woman, the man slowed down and said, "Oh Miss, you dropped this." He said in a very friendly calm voice.

She turned and was startled at first, but started toward him and said, "What did I drop?"

As they got closer together, she started to show signs of fear, because in the man's hand was a rope with handles on each end. The rope was two feet in length made of nylon. As she turned and ran, he came up on her, placed the rope around her neck and pulled her hard to the ground.

The force brought her feet off the ground and slammed her to the concrete. As she struggled, he just tightened the rope, squeezing the life out of her. John Doe watched her die with a paralyzing smile on his empty face.

He removed the rope and placed it in his pocket. He then used a pair of scissors and carefully cut a lock of her hair. He coiled it up and carefully placed it into a bag. The man stood over her poking her face with the same smile on his sick face when he was a boy. He stood up and walked out of the alley whistling a tune.

Wally's heart was racing as he watched the man walk down the street after this brutal murder, as if nothing happened. As he walked, Wally could see everything that the man was seeing…the tall buildings, the sound of light city traffic. The man stopped at a major street corner and to Wally's disbelief, he recognized the street sign, Michigan Avenue and Chestnut. Wally saw all of the familiar buildings and stores and knew just where the man was.

As the man walked east on Chestnut, Wally could see every detail, every person who passed this man smiled because of his happy disposition and nature. How could he still be smiling and whistling?

The man stopped in front of a beautiful brownstone apartment building and walked in. Wally could clearly see the address on a bronze plate on the side of the building.

The address read: 1107 Chestnut.

"Hey Wally are you ready to go back?" Bob asked as he entered the morgue.

Wally looked at Bob with a chill still running through his bones and said,

"Sure, let's go, I've seen enough here."

Bob walked up to Wally as he was sliding John Doe back and closing the stainless refrigerator door marked F-1.

"Sure is sad that this poor bastard has no name. You like you've seen a ghost. Wally, are you ok?" Bob asked as they walked toward the elevator.

"I'm fine. I guess the pathologist put a little too much formaldehyde in the chest cavity. It made me a little queasy," Wally murmured.

"Well, the fresh air will do you good. Hey, I'm starved. How does Mexican sound?" Bob asked as they headed for the car.

"I'm not really hungry. How about stopping at Taco Bell and ordering at the drive-thru? I'll just get a coke," Wally said still thinking about what he had seen.

"Great, that sounds great. There is one on the way home," Bob said.

Bob pulled up to the drive-thru and ordered 5 beef burritos and two large soft drinks. On the drive home, Bob did all the talking as he wolfed down the burritos. Wally just sat in the car thinking about what he had experienced. Wally felt as though he had to tell someone, but not Bob. He knew he could tell Helen; but the logical person to confide in was Max.

As Wally walked into the house, he was greeted by Helen with a kiss.

"How was your day with Bob at St. Vincent's? Did you solve the mysteries?" She asked.

Wally looked at the boys in the family room and said to Helen. "No it's a dead end, a wasted trip." He did not want the boys to hear what had happened. He would tell Helen in private after he spoke to Max. This little white lie was not a marriage breaker.

Wally called Max's office and his secretary mentioned that Max would be gone all day. Wally then called Max's house. Teresa answered.

"Hello, Wally. How are you?" she asked.

"Oh fine, Teresa. When will Max be home?" Wally said in a somewhat troubled voice.

"About 6:30 tonight… is everything OK?" Teresa asked in a concerned voice.

"Oh, everything is fine, honest. Would you just have him call me the second he steps into the house, please?" Wally asked still sounding troubled.

"I sure will, Wally. Can I be of some help?" She asked.

"I'm sorry if I sound a little crazy. I've spent the day with Bob Willis and you know what a nut he is," Wally said forcing a laugh.

"I will give him the message as soon as he hits the door. Hey, is Helen handy?" she asked.

"Sure, I will get her." Wally called for Helen to pick up the phone. Wally knew when Helen and Teresa got on the phone, it could be for hours. He couldn't quite understand what they could possibly talk about.

Wally went into the TV room to see what the boys were watching.

"Hey guys, what's going on?" Wally asked.

"Hi, Dad…our teacher said that the police found a dead guy near town. Are you going to get him? Was he shot?" Jeremy asked.

"Yes, son. They did find a man dead in a field next to Highway forty-one." Wally said.

"Where was he shot, Dad?" Sammy asked.

"Boys, this is not a great thing to be talking about. The police don't know anything yet," Wally said.

"Does his family know yet?" Jeremy asked.

"Boys, you two sure ask a lot of question. What are you watching?" Wally said in a somber voice, trying to get John Doe off of his mind.

Oh, some dumb western," Sammy said.

The phone rang and Wally raced to it.

"DeVere Funeral Home, Wally speaking," he said.

"Wally, this is Franny Smithe. Bill just passed away at the county hospital.

"I am so sorry, Franny. I know Bill fought a long battle with cancer. I'm sure he is at peace now. Are you at the hospital?" Wally said in a comforting voice.

"Yes, I'm with my kids and grandchildren. He got to see everybody before he died." Franny said as she started to weep.

"I will be right over, hon." As Wally started out the door, the phone rang. It was Max.

"Wally, Teresa says you act as though you have killed someone. What that hell is going on my friend? Asked Max.

"Oh damn, Max. I am just out the door. Bill Smithe just died at the hospital and I have to make a removal. I really need to talk to you," Wally said sounding desperate.

"What the hell's going on? You sound like a basket-case! My day is pretty shot tomorrow…"Max said as Wally cut him off short.

"Max, you are my best friend. I have to talk to you tonight. I should be finished with Mr. Smithe at about 10:00p.m.," Wally said.

"Ok, Ok….just come over when you flush and fill Mr. Smithe. Calm down Wally," Max said.

"Thank, see you then….you know I hate it when you disrespect the dead." Wally said.

"I'm sure that Mr. Smithe won't mind…see you when you get here my friend." Max said.

"Thanks Max." Wally said. He walked to the garage and backed the hearse out. He needed to get this out of his mind and get his game face on. The Smithe's needed 100% of me he thought.

As Wally walked to the nurses' station on the third floor, he was greeted by Franny.

"Oh, I am so glad you are here, Wally. Bill is at the end of the hall in room 107. Rev. Bob was also here when Bill passed away. He is so wonderful,"

She said as she hugged Wally.

"I am so sorry about Bill, Franny. He will never suffer again." Wally said as he hugged her.

The Smithes were very active in Wally's church.

"Fran, I will follow you to Bill," Wally said. Wally followed her to Bill's room.

Fran stood by Bill's bed and looked at her husband of sixty- five years. She held his hand and said, Good-bye, ole boy. I love and adore you….I will miss you." She said as the tears ran down her leathery cheeks.

Wally was greeted by Rev. Bob.

He looks so at peace, Wally," Franny said.

"You know, he looks pretty good. He is probably on a combine in heaven with some Red Barn chew that he had to give up some years ago." Wally said with a boyish grin.

Did you ever see him chew recently? You know how stubborn he was about change." Franny said squeezing Wally's hand.

Well, maybe once or twice when I came over for eggs." Wally said squeezing back.

The Smithe's are one of the biggest farmers in the area. Bill was eighty-seven and harvested last fall like a sixteen year old. When he visited the doctor for some dizzy spells, he was diagnosed with full-blown cancer and given two to three months to live. Bill was a very strong and proud man and it was so sad to see the cancer take a part of his life everyday.

Rev. Bob signaled to Wally that the family was ready for him to take Mr. Smithe.

"You may wait in the lobby while I take Bill in my care or stay if you wish. Most people like to leave the room, but it's what you wish." Wally said with a warm smile.

"May I stay and help you?" asked Bill's twenty year old grandson, Todd.

"Sure you may. I will welcome help with your Grandpa," Wally said as the room emptied.

Wally directed the young man to get on one side of Bill and he on the other. Wally raised toe bed level with the cot.

"I am going to slide this plastic board under your Grandpa and you will gently raise him until the board is under him. Then with your help, we will slide his sheets and your grandpa on the cot. Would you like to say a prayer before we start, Todd?" Wally asked.

"I sure would," he replied.

As Todd started the prayer, Wally placed his hand on Bill's forearm. When Wally took a deep breath, the air was a pure and as fresh as a spring breeze that warmed his heart. He saw a little white church and the doors flew open. He saw a young couple run out hand in hand.

The woman had on a white veil and the man was dressed in a dark suit. The man was tall and handsome. Her dress was as white as the first snow in November. They stopped and embraced as the people started to pour out of the church.

Wally could hear the man whisper, "I will always love you with every breath that I take for all of my life, Franny."

Wally then saw the same couple sitting under an oak tree with a pond in the background, having a picnic. He just sat gazing at his bride, stroking her hair. The love that their eyes shared was overwhelming.

Wally saw an old man in a rocking chair, whittling a piece of wood. It was the fall of the year because the west wind was blowing that brown and gold leaves from the trees.

The woman came up behind him and said, "I sure love you, my ole boy." She gently kissed him and held him with joy.

Wally opened his eyes as Todd said 'Amen.' With the help of Bill Smithes Grandson, Wally gently placed Bills body on the cot. The young man thanked Wally for allowing him to help.

Wally smiled and thanked him and said, "Todd, your grandparents have shared a wonderful life together." Wally wheeled the cot out of the room and into the hall. Franny completely lost her composure and broke down in tears. She was comforted by her children. Rev. Bob was also there every minute.

Wally put Mr. Smithe into the hearse and headed home. The hospital removal got John Doe off of Wally's mind for a moment. Wally couldn't wait to talk to talk to Max for advice and or mental help about this situation that haunts Wally.

He wanted to talk to Max before he started to embalm, but he had to focus and serve the Smithe Family. He finished Mr. Smithe at 10:15 p.m. and drove to see Max.

Max was in his study smoking a forty -dollar Cuban cigar that he got in Canada. He was also drinking an Old Style beer out of a can.

Teresa answered the door and hugged Wally. "Is everything OK with you and Helen?" she asked.

"Oh, heavens yes, Hon, we're fine. It's nothing like that." Wally said as the hug ended.

"Max is in the study. I'm so glad everything is OK," she said.

Wally walked through a beautiful sunken living room to Max's study. His study was built like Bruce Wayne's office in the series 'Batman'. Decorated in cherry paneling and trim with ornate beams on the ceiling; he even had a red phone under glass. Max is a serious attorney, but a little kid otherwise.

"How about a Monte Cristo and an Old Style, my friend? I think you need it from the sound of your voice on the phone." Max said as Wally sat down on the leather couch.

"I'll take an Old Style, but no cigar," Wally said.

"Let's cut to the chase Wally. What the fuck is going on with you?" Max asked with a big smile.

"I went to St. Vincent's with Bob Willis…" Wally said as Max interrupted.

"I would be upset if I spent the day with that jack-off," Max said.

You're right there, he did drive me crazy. Anyway, this is serious. Max please….I went with him for the John Doe investigation. Bob was supposed to meet a crime lab expert for a new DNA search," Wally said as Max interrupted.

"I think I know where this is going. Why the hell were you at the investigation? I know the drill. It's John Doe," Max said from the edge of his seat, hands folded in front of him.

"Max, please listen…I know where John Doe lives or lived." Wally said and paused.

"Oh…fuck, Jesus Christ, what the hell are you talking about? Don't give me that spiritual bullshit! What's going on with you Wally…you're acting a little Looney?" Max said as Wally quickly interrupted.

"1107 Chestnut. It's downtown Chicago…check it out, will you?" Wally said with tension in his voice.

"You mean you saw the address in one of your fucking dreams? Is that it?" Max said.

"There's more, do you want to hear it or do you want to say fuck one more time?" Wally asked.

"Ok…you have my God damn undivided attention," Max said in a calm voice as he took a big drink of his beer.

"Bob and I were upstairs at the front desk and Bob was informed that the meeting was canceled until the following day for some unknown reasons. I told Bob that I had to see John Doe to see what I had to deal with. He had no problem with that and stayed upstairs to do some paper work. I went down to the basement to the morgue like a thief in the night. I walked in and opened the refrigerated door and slid out John Doe." Wally paused for a moment, caught his breath and went on.

"I placed my hand on his cold forearm. I swear to you, I didn't think I would feel a thing. All the previous funerals were local people that I knew.

Max, I say as clear as a bell a young boy walking a dog on a leash into an alley, toss the dog over a low wire, like a telephone wire and held the leash as the dog choked to death. The boy had a smile on his face that entire time. But that's not all, Max. I then saw a man following a woman down a street and as she turned down the alley, he ran and stopped at the end of the alley right behind her. In a voice that I will never forget, he said… 'Hey Miss, you dropped something.' She turned and I don't know why she walked to him. Maybe because he was clean-cut and well dressed or he had a soft and non-threatening voice.

"Oh, I forgot, he had a rope about a foot long in his hand with handles on each end. I don't know what she saw as she walked toward him, but she freaked and turned quickly and started to run, but it was too late. He rushed up behind her and placed a rope around her neck and pulled her hard to the ground.

"Max, I watched this sick son of a bitch kill her with a smile on his face the entire time." Wally said waiting for a reaction from Max.

"Oh, shit, I don't want to believe this, but you are too great of a guy to flip out. No to fucking flip out…that is my style my friend, but not yours, Wally."

You have an address which would be an easy way for an investigation, but the way you obtained the information is a little wacky," Max said

"I know, Max, I know. Max, this guy also cut a lock of her hair and carefully put it in a baggie. I think this is not the only murder that this guy committed. I stopped the vision when Bob yelled to ask if I was ready to leave." Wally said.

"You didn't tell 'dipshit' about this did you? Oh, tell me that you didn't tell Bob, Wally?"

"No, but he sensed that something was wrong. I told him that the formaldehyde made me dizzy. He was too interested in Taco Bell to think something was wrong. Max, I feel obligated to let someone know." Wally said.

"Obligated to who…the fucker who puts you in a straight jacket! Listen to me very carefully, Wally. Do you trust me, my friend?" Max said in a calm but mythical voice.

"Why do you think I am here, Max?" Wally said.

Max stood up and got two more beers from his refrigerator that was custom built into one of the panels in his office.

"I'm going to phone Rick Lawson, who investigates white collar crime for the state police. I will give him the address and have him check it out. If it proves to be false, then no harm, no foul. If it is true…your world will be rocked my friend. Now your attorney and you are my client. Listen to me very carefully to the question that I am about to ask you. I need a simple yes or no answer only. Do you want to pursue this, Wally?" Max said with a stone face.

Wally got up…walked around the room, and looked at Max and said, 'YES!'

"Go home and get some sleep. I'll take care of everything. Don't worry. Wally. If you're right, your life will be under a magnifying glass and it will definitely change." Max said.

Wally left Max sitting in his office, sipping a whiskey. He knew of the Barber murders in the early nineties that had never been solved. He hoped his friend had not stumbled on to the biggest unsolved murders in history.

Wally went home and sat Helen down and told her about John Doe. She was a little upset because he didn't tell her first, but she understood why.

The next morning, Wally had to concentrate on the Smithe arrangements and the funeral. He knew he would not let John Doe pre-occupy his thoughts, especially now that Max was taking charge. Wally pondered over the situation. He was not sure if he wanted to be right or wrong about John Doe.

Max called Rick Lawson to come over to his office. Rick could sense in Max's voice that it was not a joking matter.

Rick had been a state police officer for over 20 years and was an investigator in the drug task force. He was tough crafty and would go undercover for months at a time, blending in with the drug dealers and the scum of the earth. He got shot while arresting a dealer and left him with a slight limp. Rick then worked with white color crime. He was investigating a doctor that was dealing in drugs. The doctor found out he was undercover and hired a bearded thug to kill him slowly. The doctor did not realize that the thug was an undercover FBI agent that was deep in cover. Rick served the doctor with thirty-eight felony counts with a grin on his face. This was the last dangerous mission of Rick's career. After the near death experience with the doctor, Rick worked at the state police post as a supervisor.

Rick and Max had been friends for years, they respected each other's brass balls and the love of the law.

"Max, what is your schedule like today or tomorrow?" Rick asked.

"I'll move my appointments today to see you." Max said.

"I have some paper work to file at the post. I can be in your office in one hour…will that work for you Max?" Rick asked.

"Great, see you in an hour," Max said as he hung up the phone.

Max had instructed his secretary to interrupt him as soon as Rick arrived.

"Tell Rick that I will be five minutes. I'm finishing up with a client," Max said over the intercom to his secretary.

"Your boss drags me into his office and now makes me wait." Rick said laughing.

"Well, you know how Max is." She said.

"Oh, I know him too well!"

Rick heard the door open and a voice yelling, "Get back here."

He walked into Max's office and sat down.

"Where's the God-damn fire, Maxxy?" Rick asked, not getting a reaction from Max.

"Listen, I represent a client who gave me some information about a John Doe. I need a favor. If this pans out, you will get my clients name. If not, no name and no harm done. This is just kind of a crazy hunch…do we have an agreement?' Max said in a stern voice

"Sure, Max," Rick said confused.

"Now don't say a fucking thing…just listen. I want you to check a brown stone apartment building in Chicago. Just check it out and call me. OK? I know how you are, asshole, just check it out and call…clear!" Max said very sternly.

"Where is your sense of humor, Max? Did you leave it in your wife's new Jaguar?" Rick said to lighten the moment.

"Rick…this is a friend of mine." Max said in an almost whisper.

"OK, OK, just give me the information." Rick said.

"Check out 1107 Chestnut. I called on the address and it's a swank multi-unit condo near Water tower Place. My client thinks John Doe lives or lived there." Max said.

"But Max…" Rick said as Max quickly interrupted.

"Just check out the God-damn build and call me, OK." Max said as he walked Rick out of his office, practically pushing him out the door.

Rick left Max's office very confused. The State Police and the FBI used all of their tactics to find the identity of John Doe. How did Max's client know all this, unless he knew the guy? He wasted no time on the lead. He stopped by the post for the file on John Doe and headed for Chicago.

Rick did not investigate this case, so he was not familiar with it. He studied the report and file and all the pictures of John Doe.

He got on Michigan Ave. and headed north to Chestnut. He headed east and found the brownstone. Rick circled that neighborhood to find a parking space. He was too cheap to pay ten dollars to park. He finally found a spot and walked back to 1107 Chestnut.

The build was a beautiful old landmark. The lobby had rich marble floors and was decorated with plush furniture and furnishings. It also had a security guard in a red and gold uniform with tails. Rick thought he was in London.

"May I assist you, sir?" asked the condo security guard.

"Yes, I am Lt. Lawson from the Indiana State Police. We are investigating a John Doe who was murdered and dumped in a cornfield in Indiana. Have you noticed if any of your tenants have disappeared in the last week or so?" Rick asked.

"Sir, people come and go quite often. This is a very exclusive building. Do you have a warrant?" the guard said in a pompous manner.

"No, I don't, but I could quickly get one if you wish." Rick said sharply.

"Then I suggest you get one and leave the property, good day Lt." he said.

"Listen, to solve this quickly and to make me go away, could I just ask you to look at a picture for identification please, and I will be on my way? Rick said.

"Oh…very well, I know everyone in the building, let's take a look." The guard said with curiosity.

All Rick had to do was hold the picture up of the corpse to the guard's face.

"Oh, my God, that's Mr. Salvitor, Ross Salvitor. Oh, how horrible," he said in confusion.

"He lives in this building?" Rick asked his heart racing.

"Why yes, in number 2107 facing the lake," the security guard said still in shock.

"May I use your phone?" Rick asked.

"Most certainly," the security guard said.

Rick called the post commander and was told to sit tight. A homicide detective and the FBI would be right there.

"I haven't seen Mr. Salvitor for some time, but he travels quite frequently. He was such a nice man. Who would want to kill him?" he said.

Detective Ryan, who was with the Chicago Police Department, showed up at the scene first.

"Do you have a key to Mr. Salvidor's apartment?" Ryan asked.

"Why yes. I have the keys to all of the units, locked up in our office. Do you want me to let you in?" the guard said anxiously.

"Not yet, we are waiting for a search warrant. Who are you?" Ryan asked Lawson.

"I am Lt. Lawson from the Indiana State Police. I was told by a local attorney that his client knew the address of a John Doe, which turns out to be Mr. Salvitor's address.

A street cop in blues delivered the search warrant from Judge Posh. The security guard told them that he would have maintenance let them into the apartment.

"He will meet you on the 21st floor," the guard said.

The three men got on the elevator and pressed 21. They were greeted by the building maintenance man.

"This way, gentleman," he said.

The men followed him to 2107.

"Mr. Salvitor was such a nice man, who would want to kill him?" he asked as he unlocked the door with a shaky hand.

As the door opened, the men entered and stood in the foyer, all eyes circling this lavishly beautiful apartment. It was furnished in fine African mahogany and carved imported walnut furniture, beautiful oriental rugs, and the walls were adorned with beautiful oil paintings and tapestries. Nothing was out of place…

The dining room had a large glass and brass table with ten leather high back chairs around it. There was a beautiful fourteenth century ornate roll top desk nearby with mail neatly stacked on top.

The kitchen was spotless, with white cabinets, white tile floor and appliances that would cost more than the average home in Goodland. There was not a dish, glass or crystal stemware out of place.

They walked down the hallway past two bedrooms and into the master-suite, which was like a scene from 'Lifestyles of the Rich and Famous." It contained a custom bed the size of Wrigley Field. Two Louis VIII high-boy dressers and two oversized stuffed leather chairs and a walk-in closet that you could get lost in.

A beautiful balcony led off the master bedroom and there was another balcony as well off the living room. Both face Lake Michigan.

"Let's start in the guy's bedroom. He has to have some dirty little secrets," Ryan said.

"Look at this guy's wardrobe. I bet this guy has fifty some suits and a hundred pair of shoes, some still with store tags. This suit must have cost over two thousand dollars. I only have 2 suits to my name." Lawson said.

The men started to do a routine search, all in rubber gloves, to try to discover some reason behind the shooting of Ross Salvidor.

"What does this guy do for a living?" asked Lt. Lawson.

"We're running a social security check on him. We don't know yet," Ryan answered.

"Hey, I think I found something, Detective Ryan," the policeman shouted.

Both Ryan and Lawson came running to the bedroom closet. He had found two Cole Hahn shoe boxes with baggies full of what looked to be human hair. The hair was neatly coiled up in each bag.

"This guy must have been some kind of hairdresser. Look at all these bags of hair," the officer said.

"Holy shit, this can't be the Barber murderer that we have been hunting for over fifteen years?" Ryan asked in disbelief.

The men counted 2wenty-seven bags of hair.

"Who is the Barber murderer?" the officer asked.

"Boy, you must be new on the force. In 1989, we started to find dead woman who were strangled. The murderer would always take a lock of his victim's hair. My God, this makes perfect sense. The murders were committed from 1989 to 1994. I was on the case. Twenty-three confirmed murders all done in the same manner." Detective Ryan said.

"There are twenty-seven bags of hair. How do you explain that?" the police officer asked.

"Well, maybe this sick bastard was on vacation and brought four souvenirs home with him," Ryan answered in a sarcastic tone.

Ryan phoned the police chief and in minutes the building was swarming with Chicago policemen. The Illinois crime lab was searching every inch of the apartment.

"What's the story with the attorney whose client identified Salvitor. I want him in my office at once. We will get a subpoena if we have to." Ryan said to Lawson.

"I don't know that whole story, but I will contact the attorney at once." Lt. Lawson said.

"Sir, we found a hidden safe build in the wall in a closet," one of the investigating officers said.

"Well, open the fucking thing, God-damn it. Get a lock-smith down here at once." Ryan demanded.

The lock was drilled out and everyone stood around him when the safe was slowly opened.

The others moved back so that Ryan could reach into the safe. He pulled out stacks of case, documents, and a solid gold Rolex. In the back of the safe was a large velvet pouch with several pads of paper or journals. Detective Ryan pulled out one of the note pads and started to read. The room was silent as Ryan's eyes enlarged.

"Oh, this sick bastard!...Boys!...We have the Barber murderer, too bad the prick is dead. Get me that fucking attorney and his client from Indiana!" Ryan shouted.

CHAPTER 10

Teresa walked to answer the phone, "Hello, Goldburg residence," she said.

"Is Max there, please? It's Rick Lawson, I tried his office," he said out of breath for all the excitement.

"No, he is taking a deposition at Doug Block's office. What's wrong?" She asked sensing the tension in his voice.

"Oh, no big deal. I'm just trying to get some information about a bad guy to him," said Rick.

After talking to Teresa, he phoned the post and had them patch him through to the law office where Max was conducting the deposition.

"Tyson, Block and Leer. May I help you?" a receptionist asked.

"Yes, is there a Max Goldberg there? I need to speak to him," Lawson said sharply.

"He is in a deposition and cannot…" she said as Lawson quickly cut her off.

"This is Lt. Richard Lawson from the Indiana State Police. I need to speak with him now. Do you understand, Miss?" Lawson said.

"Yes sir, I will get him right away," she replied.

The receptionist got out of her chair and headed for the conference room. When she told Max that a detective from the Indiana State Police wanted to speak with him and would not wait, he knew what is was about.

You can take the call from this phone," she said.

"I need privacy," Max said turning to the men in the room.

"If you all will excuse me for a moment, this is urgent." He said.

"Please follow me Mr. Goldburg; there is a phone in this vacant office. Just push line 6." She said pointing to the office space.

"This is Max, speaking." He said

"Max, it's Rick. Your John Doe information was correct. This asshole is the Barber Murderer. We found evidence linking him to the murders. Your client has some explaining to do. Get him to my office or..." Rick said Max cut him off.

"Wait a minute, Rick. This is my client. Do not give me orders and settle down. My client is not a God-damn criminal and he will not be treated like one. He is an outstanding citizen. Let me talk to him and we will cooperate fully with you. You have my word on it, OK Rick?" Max said with conviction.

"OK, I'm just a little edgy; page me when you talk to him Max. This is not to be leaked out about the Barber murders. I do not want the press to get the information. With all due respect Max, the FBI and Chicago police want some answers yesterday...if you know what I mean," Rick said.

"Don't worry, my lips are sealed. I will get back to you ASAP." Max said as he hung up the phone. He has a sick feeling about what was in store for his friend Wally.

He finished his deposition. He wanted to personally talk to Wally. His mind was racing on the drive home. He dictated several memos to prepare for his conversation with Wally and the police. Max walked to the door and rang the bell.

"Hello Max, did you find out..." asked Wally as Max cut him off.

"Let's talk," Max said as they went into Wally's office.

"Was the address right?" Wally asked.

"Wally, please shut up my friend. I'll talk. You were right; the stiff's name is Ross Salvitor. He is a fucking mass murderer, who was called the Barber murderer. He allegedly has killed over twenty-five women. Wally, I have known you for a long time and I believe you; but the police will interrogate the living shit out of you. They will probably be sticking a microscope up your butt to find answers. Wally this is big news. It will also draw national attention. It will be very difficult for you, Helen and the boys.

"This Murderer stalked the woman of Chicago between about 1989 and 1995. The police had what they believe were twenty-three confirmed murders blamed on him based on the similar MO's.

The women were all in their twenties to mid-thirties and all had hair cut from their heads. At the address that you gave me, the police found twenty-seven baggies full of human hair. They are checking DNA for matches.

There were also journals found. This sick fuck described every detail of every murder. This guy loved to kill. Wally…the Chicago police and the FBI want to speak to you at once." Max said.

"Why is this happening to me, who am I? Oh, Max…what am I going to do?" Wally said with his elbows on his knees and his face in his hands.

"It will be OK, I will schedule an interview tomorrow morning," Max said as Wally interrupted him.

"I have a 9:00a.m. arrangement with the Smithe Family. I will not sacrifice my families that I serve," Wally said.

"OK, I will schedule the meeting for later. Now listen to me very carefully. You might be taken into custody, just be prepared. When is the funeral? Be ready to call another funeral director, if you are incarcerated!" Max said in a stern tone.

"Are you kidding? This is not funny Max!" Wally asked.

Wally, I am not kidding. This is a very serious matter and the police are taking it very seriously also." Max said

"I didn't do anything. Why am I on trial here?" Wally said as he stood up.

"Wally, calm down, I know the law, and I am very familiar with the way the police think. They will not understand or want to understand your explanation. Who else knows about your 'voodoo power?' Max said with a forced grin.

"Let's see, Helen knows…you …Teresa and I have talked to Rev. Bob as well." Wally said.

"OK, I'm going to set up a meeting for 1:00 p.m. in my office. Call Rev Bob, and I want you and Helen and Bob in my office in one hour. I will have Teresa there too. Wally, it will be OK…you're a hero.

You discovered one of the most brutal murderers on the planet." Max said as he got up from his chair.

"I certainly don't feel like a hero, Max," Wally said as a tear ran down his cheek. Max walked Wally to his car.

Wally and Helen arrived at Max's office shortly before the hour. They were greeted by Teresa, who hugged them.

"How terrible for you Wally, but it will be fine,' Teresa said in a somber voice.

"Come on back," Max yelled from his office. They all walked in and sat around the conference table.

"Where is Rev. Bob?" Max asked.

"We tried to contact him at the church and also his home, but we were unable to contact him," Wally said.

"Shit, we need him here. I'll try. What his number?" Max asked. Wally gave the number to him as he dialed.

"Hey preacher, it's Max Goldburg. How are you? I need some salvation." Max said with a chuckle.

"There is no salvation for you, Max." Rev. Bob fired back with a laugh.

"I have a situation here and I need your services. Could you come right over to my office, please?" Max asked.

"Why, I suppose, I have a pot pie in the oven." Rev. Bob said.

"Just throw it in the refrigerator. I'll order a pizza. See you here," Max said.

Teresa ordered a pizza and some soft drinks.

"We will get started. I have a Verna Delbert here, who is a court reporter to take a statement for the record. You may wonder why I have asked her to be here. Well I am going to act as a prosecutor; I want you to understand how this can be twisted. You need to know what to say when you get hit with some serious question. Max said.

What do you mean Max.? Helen said.

"OK, here goes… Wally, you knew Mr. Salvitor. Maybe you even killed him or had him killed. He was going to confess and you killed him and dumped his body on your way home. You and Mr. Salvitor are the Barber murderers. I am looking for the death penalty, Judge.

Now Wally, I have been thinking about this, see how the truth can be twisted. We will do things by the book. I will dot every 'I' and cross every 'T' and everything will go smoothly." Max said as Rev Bob walked in.

"What did I miss?" Rev Bob asked.

They were all in Max's office for four hours, every detail and every angle was gone over. Max felt that he had covered all the bases for his best friend, Wally. Everyone was tired and felt relief, but there was still tension in Wally's mind about tomorrow.

Wally got up early the next morning and sat in the chapel thinking about his earlier vision and especially Ross Salvitor. He had to put on his game face and prepare for the Smithe arrangement and get through the visitation and funeral. Max had a way to analyze every angle of every situation. Wally thought that giving the address was the right thing to do, but it could be twisted into trouble for him and his family.

Wally met with the Smithe family and flawlessly made the arrangement. The calling was that night from 5:00 to 9:00 p.m. with the funeral at 2:00 p.m. the next day.

When Wally was a young boy he shot his dad's car window out with a BB gun. He had aimed at a bottle on a fence post. After he pulled the trigger and saw the damage, he knew he was in serious trouble.

We walked into the house and waited for his dad to get off of the phone.

He remembered his dad telling him to be careful when he shot his BB gun. The minutes his dad was on the phone while Wally was waiting seemed like decades.

Wally had a sick feeling in the pit of his stomach waiting for the meeting with the police at 1:00p.m., like the feeling he had waiting for his father to get off the phone.

Wally got in his Suburban at 12:30 p.m. and headed for Max's office. He knew that he would be early and wanted to get it over with. He also wanted to take Helen, but Max advised against it.

He was greeted by Max's secretary.

"Max said that you would be early and to go on back. He skipped lunch and he is waiting for you Wally." She said.

"That's not like Max to miss a meal." Wally said as she laughed.

"I could not believe it either; it's rare for him to miss his lunch." She said

Wally walked into Max's office and said, "Hey, my friend, are you ready for this?"

"The question is…are you ready and are you calm?" Max asked.

Wally sat down at the conference table staring at his best friend. The both heard a voices and the door opened. In walked Lt. Lawson, Detective Ryan and Detective Albert Gaglio. Detective Gagilio had been assigned to the Barber Murders from day one, which was back in November of 1984.

All of the leads and tips were dead ends. Then the killing stopped a few years ago. He was looking forward to this day for well over a decade.

The men were greeted and sat down at the conference table.

Lt. Lawson knew Wally and could not understand why the local funeral director was at the table.

"Gentleman, are we all here, shall we get started?" Max asked as he was interrupted by Lawson.

"Max, where is your client, and why is Wally here?" Lawson asked in quite a loud voice.

"Let's calm down, Rick. I will explain." Max said.

Wally felt the uneasiness of everyone in the room. This is not what I expected at all. The police officers all sat still while Max prepared to speak.

"This is not an ordinary situation. Let me explain the circumstances in the identification of John Doe, as Mr. Ross Salvitor. My client is here. It is Wally Touch, now…" Max said as he was interrupted.

Detective Gaglio stood up with fire in his eyes. He reached in his pocket for a white folded document and slammed it on the table.

"Wally Touch, I have a warrant for your arrest and I am taking you to Cook County jail to wait your arraignment. You have the right to remain silent…" Gaglio said as Max stood up and interrupted.

"Wait a God-damn minute, you are in my office. You will listen to me." Max shouted.

"You… you listen to me! I am taking your client into my custody and if you so much as interfere; I will arrest you for obstruction of justice! Clear! You can read this warrant, everything is on order." Gaglio said.

"Max, what's going on here? Wally said with tears running down his face.

Gaglio placed Wally's hands behind his back and read him his rights as he tightened the handcuffs.

"It will be alright, say nothing until I get there….where are you taking him?" Max asked Gaglio.

"Cook County jail and then to Michigan City Prison where we will fry his ass." Gaglio said with a snicker.

Max ignored the comment, "Wally, it will be alright, have faith. I will follow them and get you out, my friend." Max said with conviction.

"He won't be going anywhere, I can assure you." Gaglio said.

"One more comment like that from you, Gaglio…and I will knock you on your fucking ass. You are still in my office, is that clear, you piece of shit!" Max shouted getting right up in Gaglio's face.

Gaglio had little respect for attorneys and thought they were all wimps. He could tell that Max was very serious and his statement was not a threat but a fact.

Max's secretary gasped as Wally was escorted out of the office in handcuffs.

"Max, what is going on?" She asked.

"Just shut up and get Teresa on the phone. Tell her to get to Wally's home at once. Then call Helen and tell her that I will be right over." Max shouted as he pointed at Gaglio.

Now, Gaglio! I want to warn you right now that you are making a big mistake," Max said as he approached the unmarked car, where Wally had been placed in the back seat.

"I have been waiting over fifteen years for this. Now back off counselor!" Gaglio exclaimed with his finger poking Max's chest.

"If your finger makes contact with my chest one more time, I will break it off and shove it up your ass. This ain't Chicago, you're in my town!" Max screamed.

"Get in the God-damn car Gaglio, he means it!" Lawson said as Gaglio got into the car.

Max did not like the situation that Wally was in. He stood there rubbing his head in anger as the car sped off and out of sight.

"Could you loosen these handcuffs, please?" Wally asked sobbing.

"Shut up, you fucking baby. I hope your hands fall off. I have been waiting my whole career for this, you scumbag. I would like to break your fucking jaw right now." Gaglio said.

"Back-off, leave this man alone. Remove his cuffs. I know this man and you are out of line." Lawson said sternly.

"You are out of your jurisdiction, pal." Gaglio said.

"Wally don't say a word to him." Lawson said as he started to take the cuffs off.

"No, they stay on, Lawson. I will drop you off right here and you can walk!" Gaglio Shouted.

It was a quiet ride to Chicago. Lawson felt bad for Wally. He knew that if Wally was left alone with Gaglio, he would probably confess to anything. Gaglio wanted to rip his head off. Wally sat in terror of this. He had not even had a speeding ticket or ever been stopped by a policeman.

Helen was standing outside in tears as Max drove up.

"Where is Wally, Max? What's going on?" Helen asked in hysterics.

Max got out of his car and held Helen.

"There has been a grave misunderstanding. It will be alright. Teresa is on her way right now to watch the boys so you and I can go to Chicago." Max said.

"I love Wally more than life, but I am so upset with him for getting involved in this." She said. She could not stop crying and the trip north seemed never ending for them both.

CHAPTER 11

There was very little conversation on the drive to Chicago. Max tried to keep Helen Calm. He focused his thoughts on the situation and how a hungry district attorney will react to Wally's story.

When Gaglio brought Wally into Cook County jail for processing, every piercing eye was focused on Wally. He was printed and booked like a common street thug. He was then placed in a cell. Wally paced the cell like a caged tiger. He pleaded for the jailer to tell him what was happening, but no answers were given to him.

Max and Helen arrived and tried to post bail.

"No bail for Wally Touch… judges orders," the jail administrator said.

"I want to speak to him. I am his attorney," Max demanded as he showed his ID.

"You're an Indiana attorney. You can't practice law in Illinois, therefore you can't see him…you need to leave." The administrator said as Max fumbled through his wallet.

"Here, I am licensed in Indiana, Illinois, and Florida. Now I demand to see my client or else, and you know what or else means pal." Max said sternly.

"Wait here." He said

"I'm so afraid for Wally," Helen said as Max patted her shoulder. Wally was taken out of the cell and into a room with a steel table and two chairs. He sat and waited for Max to come in.

"I'm so glad to see you, Max. Please get me out of here… I'm so scared," Wally said as he tried to hug Max with his hands cuffed in front of him.

"Listen to me very carefully…Wally, you will be formally charged and a bail will be set. This is bull shit, but the state wants a conviction on the Barber Murders. It will be OK, Wally, I promise," Max said with a forced smile.

"Max I can't go back in there. I'm terrified. Please don't let them take me back there, please Max." Wally grimaced as he sobbed uncontrollable.

"Wally, you need to be strong right now. You will be out tomorrow and we will laugh about this someday soon." Max said, but he knew that nothing would make Wally want to laugh about this.

"How are Helen and the boys?" Wally asked wiping the tears away from his red cheeks.

"The boys are fine. Helen is in the waiting room, but they will not let her see you. Teresa is with the boys at your house. It will be fine and all over tomorrow." Max said.

"Max, I have a visitation this evening and a funeral tomorrow. I must get back. Can't you make them understand? Oh…please… get me out of here… Max…I'm begging you." Wally said with tears in his eyes.

"We called Vince Bower from my car phone. He was happy to help you with the visitation and funeral." Max said.

"He is a good funeral director. Thank you." Wally said.

"Time is up counselor," the jailer said as he walked into the holding room.

"Be strong buddy," Max said as the jailer took Wally back to his cell.

"Let me talk to the administrator, please," Max said to the desk clerk.

The jail administrator met with Max in the hallway,

"What can I do for you Mr. Goldburg?" He asked

"May I talk to you in private please?" Max asked, not wanting Helen to hear what he had to say.

"Very well, this way please." He said

"I will be a few minutes, Helen, it will be alright." Max said in a reassuring voice.

The two men walked into the administrator's office.

"Wally Touch has never had a traffic violation or been stopped by a cop. Detective Gaglio has treated him like a violent criminal. I beg of you to keep Wally on a suicide watch. He did nothing wrong and the stress behind bars could make him do something to himself. I want him protected, please." Max said.

"I understand your concern; I will move him out of a cell and into a holding room. There is a 24 hour monitor and the room is much more comfortable. The district attorney won't like it, but I will deal with him." The administrator said as he shook Max's hand.

"Thank-you," Max said as he left the office.

Helen sobbed all the way home as Max silently thought about his defense.

The next morning, Wally's picture was in every newspaper in the country and on every broadcast, linking him to the Barber Murders.

The Smithe family called Helen and said that they were calling another funeral home to pick up their father. Helen pleaded with them that it was a big mistake, but it did no good. Tower Funeral Home came to remove Mr. Smithe.

Francis was very gracious and was sorry for taking the Smithe call.

Helen and Max drove to Chicago for the arraignment. Helen sobbed as Wally was brought in handcuffs and leg irons. He had on a tight orange jumpsuit with Cook County in bold black letters across the back. Max approached the bench at the Cook County Courtroom and asked if he could speak with the District Attorney and the judge in his chambers. The request was granted.

As the three men left the courtroom, Max winked at Wally and whispered.

"Everything will be alright."

They all sat at a conference table and Max stood up.

"Gentleman, what we have is my client in handcuffs and leg irons, who solved the Barber murders. Without his contact, they would not have been solved. The warrant that was served was illegal. In your haste, you failed to get a federal warrant. You served a state warrant. We all know that was a big mistake. I did not bring this up when Detective Gaglio served it because he would have gotten a federal warrant, so I allowed Mr. Touch to be transported to your state.

We are not hiding anything, nor is Wally Touch guilty of any crime." Max stated in a calm voice.

"I am prepared to explain the circumstances that led to the identification of John Doe, who is Ross Salvitor, the most sought after serial killer since the BTK killer. Now if I may have your full attention with no interruptions until I am finished, please." Max pleaded.

"Wally has been a funeral director for sixteen years. I have personally known him all of my life. He is the kindest and most compassionate human being I have ever met. Less than a year ago, Wally purchased his funeral home from a Mr. William DeVere. Wally and his wife were not financial well off enough to purchase the funeral home, so Mr. DeVere and the bank saw to it that Wally was to be the new owner.

"You see, Mr. DeVere's wife passed away and Wally came to officiate at the service. Mr. DeVere was so impressed and happy with the care that Wally gave. His funeral home had been in his family for five generations and Mr. DeVere did not have any Aires. Wally was a perfect fit to take over such a prestigious family business.

Since taking over the DeVere funeral home, Wally discovered that he had a…let's say a gift. I don't know how to put it. Now this may sound crazy, but Wally can see the past when he touches the deceased," Max said

"You expect me to believe that hogwash?" The district attorney exclaimed.

"Well, let's put it this way, calls have been flooding my office from every network in the country. You have no evidence and can only hold my client for seventy-two hours without probable cause. Wally is guilty of giving you your unsolved murders and you treat him like a criminal. You can investigate Wally Touch all you like and you will find nothing. Please release my client," Max begged.

"I still would like to hold him for seventy-two hours to investigate his where abouts during the murders and Mr. Salvitor's murder." The DA said.

Max pulled out a file from his briefcase and tossed it on the conference table.

"I have already done that for you. It's all in the file, Wally's whereabouts on the times in question. Again, please judge…he is an upstanding citizen, release him," Max again said

"Mr. Goldburg is right. You have no solid evidence on this man. I am releasing him. If you find some solid information on Mr. Touch, I will look at it. I do not see him as a flight risk." Said the judge.

"What about bail in case he flees to…" The DA said as the judge interrupted.

"I don't think Mr. Touch is the type to flee. I have made my decision." The judge said.

"Thank-you, your honor," Max said as the district attorney stomped out of the room.

As the judge and Max entered the courtroom, Max gave Wally a wink and a smile.

"Could the bailiff please remove the handcuffs and leg irons from Mr. Touch"? I am granting a release of Mr. Touch. The District Attorney will review your file and is still investigating this matter. You are free to go." The judge said as he waited for Max, Helen and Wally to clear the courtroom before hearing the next case.

Wally embraced Helen while Max patted them both on the back. Max noticed that the District Attorney was not amused with the ruling.

"Let's get your clothes and you can turn this fashionable outfit in, unless you want it when you do yard work around the funeral home." Max said with a smile.

"No, I think not, they can keep this monkey suit." Wally said pulling at the jump suit.

Helen and Max waited for Wally to check out of the Hilton with bars. They walked outside to get to their car and were swarmed by the press.

"The state of Illinois found no information to keep Wally Touch. His only crime was to lead the police to the Barber Murderer; for without Wally, these brutal murders could have gone unsolved. Thank-you." Max spoke frankly before they got into the car.

The press was hungry for more information, but that was all that they would get for now.

"Thank-you Max, I could not stand another minute in that place. I don't care if I ever come back to Chicago. How was the Smithe funeral, Helen? Did they understand?" Wally asked.

Wally, the Smithe's called the Tower Funeral Home and Frances came and picked up Mr. Smithe. He had the funeral. I'm so sorry." Helen said knowing that losing the funeral would crush Wally.

"What happened? I had everything arranged." Wally asked as Max interrupted him.

"Wally, your face was in every newspaper and broadcast in every country. Goodland is full of reporters and news vans. The story was that you were linked to the murders," Max said.

"Oh my God! What is going on here? What do I do?" Wally asked in tears, as Helen rubbed his shoulders and neck.

"Wally, please be strong and calm. You must stay focused. We are going to your home to try and sort this out. We have to prepare a statement for the press. We have a PR problem here. Some will think you are the second coming of Christ and others will think you are linked to some satanic cult. This fence will take some time to mend." Max said.

"I love you Wally, It will be fine," Helen said

"How was the Cook county jail food?" Max asked to try and cheer up his best friend.

"I let Bubba have my desert…I'm really scared, guys," Wally replied not happy with Max's jail humor.

I have had calls from The Today Show, Oprah, and even Jerry Springer. I think we should start with Jerry; he is doing a show called 'have you hugged your mass murderer today," Max said trying to keep a straight face and bursting out in laughter.

"You're a bad boy Max." Helen said

"No dear, at a time like this, he is a fucking asshole!" Wally said chuckling.

"I will take that as a compliment. It's good to see a smile on your face, little buddy." Max said.

The three discussed the situation. Max knew a political public relations expert that was very willing to get involved. As they approached Goodland, Wally seemed nervous. There was a news truck at the convenience store.

"OK, we will go to my house. The boys are already there, probably eating candy and smoking my Cubans. You need a shower and rest. We will begin tomorrow morning," Max said.

Max knew that his long driveway with a "no trespassing" sign would keep a nosey newspaper reporter back. They had a lot of planning to do. They pulled up the long drive and into the garage with the door closing behind them.

"I feel like a prisoner. I can't even go anywhere right now without being stalked," Wally said as they got out of the car.

"Are you comparing my home to Cook county Jail? Max asked as he perched his eyebrow.

"You know what I mean," Wally replied as the boys ran into the garage and hugged their dad.

They went into the kitchen and were greeted by Teresa who was wearing an apron.

"Oh Wally we were so worried about you." She said as she hugged him.

"Something smells great," Wally said

"I'm making a French casserole. I got the recipe out of Cosmo. Teresa said as Helen joined her at the sink and helped her with the lettuce for the salad.

"I get a little nervous when Teresa cooks something new," Max said with a smile.

"I will remember that when you take a second helping, buster," Teresa sternly said.

They sat around the dining room table and entertained by Max. He knew that he had to keep the evening light to avoid thinking about the situation at hand.

Max didn't want Wally to know that the townspeople of Goodland thought that Wally was involved in the murders. They were angry about what they didn't know. Max had his phone calls transferred to his office to avoid an abundance of calls.

Max knew that the judge would voice a "no comment" to the press, but he did not know what the District Attorney would say.

They would all know in the morning when the Chicago Sun Times was delivered.

The boys went to bed early. They slept in a spare bedroom that Max called the "hunt room." Max had a deer and a bobcat mounted on the walls as well as several other wildlife displays. The wall paper in the room was an English hunt scene. The boys thought the room was cool.

Wally and Helen soon turned in and Max quickly turned on Channel 5 to see the news about his best friend. Max was relieved that the conversation with the District Attorney outside the courtroom was not harmful. He simply said that no charges were filed against Wally Touch, linking him to the Barber murders and to the death of Ross Salvitor. Further investigations of Mr. Touch were still ongoing.

Max could live with Wally being investigated, but not with him being considered as a suspect. Max turned off the TV and cracked open an Old Style and stared out the front windows at the news trucks parked on the road. Tomorrow could not come soon enough.

Max set the alarm for 5:30 a.m. to get several newspapers and doughnuts for his guests. As he backed out of the garage a reporter and a cameraman were in his face.

"Can you give us some information about your client, Wally Touch? " The reporter asked as Max pushed the microphone out of his face.

"I will say this very calmly and clearly. I will assume that you did not see my 'No Trespassing' sign. I am going into my home and get my Winchester model 93 and if you are still in my yard, I will shoot both of you, not to kill you but to wound ." Max said in a soft voice.

He got out of the car and walked toward the garage door. The reporter and cameraman started to run for the road. Max walked in the house to watch them scurry off.

"Hey, I heard the door slam." Wally said.

"Yes, you did. I had to persuade reporters to vacate my property to avoid violence!" Max said with a big grin.

"Where are you going?" Wally asked rubbing the sleep out of his eyes.

"I'm going to town to get some doughnuts and a newspaper. I'll be right back."

"Do you want some company? I'll get dressed. Wally asked

"No, you stay here. I don't want you to be seen until we make a statement, OK." Max said as he headed for the door for the second time this morning.

As he left his long drive, he noticed news vans lined up and down the road in all directions. As he headed for town, reporters were trying to take pictures and any information, but Max was the wrong person to get to slow down.

Max drove past the funeral home before his usual bakery run. There were several TV and radio vans and a CNN tower truck. Max then pulled up in front of the bakery. He never realized that so many people were up at this hour.

He walked in and ordered two dozen assorted doughnuts.

"Max, what did Wally do? What's going on around here? How could he? A man at the counter asked as everyone waited for Max's answer.

Max turned and looked at every person in the bakery.

"Why don't you all get a rope and come over to my home and hang Wally in my back yard?" Max said as he picked up his doughnuts and coffee and headed for the checkout line. He walked across the street to the service station and bought several newspapers. All of the papers linked Wally to the Barber murders. Max slowly drove past the news trucks sipping his fresh coffee.

He walked into the kitchen and found Wally, Helen and Teresa sitting at the kitchen table.

"Teresa, my dear…Good morning. This is the first time I have ever seen you this early in the morning. I have two dozen assorted doughnuts. No one touches the cream filled ones, they have my name on them," Max said leaning over to kiss his bride as she rolls her eyes in disgust.

Max put the newspaper on the table as he grabbed a cream filled doughnut. Wally picked up the Indianapolis Star and started to read.

"Oh my God, the paper says that I am linked to all the murders." Wally moaned.

"Read on. It says that you are cleared of any involvement, but you are still being investigated. We were contacted by NBC and we need to get you on the Today show. I would like to be on tomorrow to get the story straight. Do you want to hear something funny? I got a call from Johnny Cochran's law offices. They want to represent you." Max said as he bit into a cream-filled doughnut.

Brad Funk, a political public relations specialist, was going to help Wally with the press and Brad was due to arrive as Max's shortly after sunrise. Max had all the confidence in the world in Brad. They attended Indiana University together and Max had marveled at his talents and political candidates that he represented throughout his career. January is not a high demand time for Brad and he was happy to do a favor for an old friend.

The boys got up and joined them for breakfast.

"I do not think it is a good idea for the boys to go to school today. Let the dust settle. You guys don't mind playing hooky today, do you?" Max asked.

"Wow, nice digs. I guess by the look of things that law has been very, very good to you," Brad said as he looked around.

"Brad, you know Teresa. Meet our good friends, Wally and Helen Touch," Max said.

"I am pleased to meet the two of you," Brad said as they went into the living room.

Brad is a tall and thin man, dressed in an oxford button down shirt, flannel pants, wire rim glasses, three button tweed coat and sporting a bowtie. This was the look of Boston not Goodland. You could tell by Brad's presence that he was mythical in thought and action. Brad would let you feed him information without even asking for it.

"Did you notice all of the media trucks, Mr. Funk?" Wally asked.

"Please call me Brad, relax…yes, I did notice the media attention to your alleged involvement. Your funeral home…I took the liberty and ran a credit check through a banking institution. You have A-1 credit. You are never late with payments. I also checked the Bureau of Motor Vehicles and you have no moving violation or a record of being stopped. You are a bloody boy scout, for God's sake. Now, Wally, tell me about you, then we will talk about what's happening now, OK?" Brad said with a smile.

Wally talked about his parents, his childhood, schooling and sports. He talked about old girlfriends that raised Helens eyebrow. He also talked about college and mortuary school. Wally gave everything to Brad except his blood type. He was a little confused about information that he felt was useless, but his respect for Brad made him keep feeding him information. Every time Wally would pause and ask if he had enough information, Brad would ask for more. Brad had a photographic memory and wrote down little.

They took a break for lunch. "You're right, Max. We need to get Wally on the today show and maybe 60 minutes. I will make the proper calls and make sure who the other guest with Wally will be. I do not want the District Attorney to blind side us. We will demand the Q and A before the show or no deal?" Brad said.

"What is Q and A, Brad? Wally asked.

"Oh. I'm sorry, it means Questions and Answers," Brad said.

"Do you know T and A is Brad?" Max said with a serious expression.

"No, Max, I am afraid that I haven't heard of T and A," Brad answered

"It's tits and ass, Brad, tits and ass!!!" Max said with a roar of laughter.

"Max, you have not changed a bit, still the pervert," Brad said shaking his head.

"Wally, are you ok with going on the air tomorrow?" Brad asked.

"You don't even know what happened to me in jail," Wally said.

"Wally I work with a lot of politicians. Trust is the core of success between my clients and myself. If you go to church with your family in the morning and you're with your mistress that afternoon and tell me. I'm OK and we can contain the problem or make the bad go away. But if you fail to tell me and I find out that you lied or left out crucial information that can slander you, game over….you lose. I have walked out on a few clients that chose to cover up something and not let me know. I am not your conscience; I am here to fix the leak. I have listened to you for four hours and you are going to do fine. You will make this situation that began as a lemon and make it into lemonade. I'm hungry, lets eat," Brad said.

"Teresa will go get us some sandwiches," Max said.

"No, you, Wally and I need to go to a high profile restaurant. Wally needs to see the intensity of the media. I will answer their questions. You just be yourself to your friends and the town's people," Brad said as they got into Max's Range Rover.

"Is this going to be costly, I mean what will this representation cost?" Wally asked concerned.

"Don't you worry, little buddy, Illinois fucked up and served you an illegal warrant. That mistake should pay for my legal fees and maybe another home in West Palm." Max said with a big grin.

"NBC, CBS, CNN should more than cover my fees. You see, networks, do not usually pay for their interviews, but they pay expenses, just refer to me as an expense. I could go for some Chinese," said Brad.

"There are no Chinese restaurants in town. We do, however, have a restaurant called Crosscourt where most of the business people eat. You will like this place Brad," Max said.

"We will eat there then, if that's alright with everyone," Brad said.

As they parked the car and started to walk to the restaurant, several reporters and cameramen swarmed the three men.

"Are you the Barber Murderer?" a reporter shouted with several more shouting questions in the background.

"Please, please, please, quiet…I will be more than happy to answer any of your questions. I am Bradley Funk and I am Mr. Touch's spokesperson." He said.

"Can you tell us about the murders?" A reporter shouted.

"No, Mr. Touch knows nothing about the so-called Barber murders. Next Question." Bradley said.

"Did Wally kill Mr. Salvator?" Asked another reporter.

"My, my, where did you get your information, from the National Enquirer?

Wally did not know Mr. Salvator before his body was found, so I guess that would rule him out as a murderer. Wally is a fine, law abiding, God fearing neighbor here in Goodland. I will have a formal statement in front of Mr. Goldburg's office at 6:00 p.m. Thank-You." Brad said as the three men entered the restaurant.

The reporters were still firing off questions in the background. Every eye was on the three men. They were seated and the waitress brought them water and a menu.

"Hi Wally, I'll give you folks a few minutes to look over the menu," she said as if she had seen a ghost.

"I'm fine Norma, thank you for asking," Wally said with a forced smile.

"Wally just relax. This is good that we are here. Everyone is curious about what they have read about you," Brad said.

"This is the biggest thing that has ever happened in Goodland since Mabel Trickleman shot her husband. Mabel shot him in the foot when she caught him in bed with Alice... Oh, I forgot her last name. The funny thing is that Mabel was aiming at Vern's balls." Max said laughing.

"Johnson, it was Alice Johnson, "Wally said with a blank stare.

"We will prepare a statement and deliver it at six in the evening. That will give the Today Show plenty of time to prepare for your interview tomorrow," Brad said as the waitress came for their orders.

"Have you gents decided what you want?" Norma asked with her pen and pad ready.

Brad and Wally ordered the Julian Salad while Max ordered a half-pound burger, fries and a chocolate milkshake.

"Max, your eating habits have not changed since college, you should donate your stomach to science, let them be amazed," Brad said as the waitress plopped down the half-pound burger in front of Max.

"Bradley, I love my wife and my Old Style beer, but I would give them both up if they got in the way of me and this burger." Max said as he bit into the massive sandwich.

They finished their meal with every eye in the place glued to their table. Wally paid for the lunch and they walked out of the door. The press was gathered outside, waiting for Wally. They started to shout questions and Bradley put both hands in the air to quiet them down. He waited until the roar of the press was still and quiet.

"Ladies and Gentlemen, we will have a formal statement at 6:00 p.m. this evening. We will happily answer any of your questions at that time. Thank-you," Brad said as they got into Max's Range Rover.

"The press is like a virus, once it gets under your skin, it spreads, festers and multiplies. It does not matter who it attacks just as long as it is breathing. When your immune system is down or your story is newsworthy look out, they will storm your system; even kill you and move on to the next breathing soul. Well, consider, I'm the doctor and you will get the first real dose of medicine at 6:00 pm this evening. This is a pretty big virus. It will take several treatments….and this virus will go away." Brad said squeezing Wally's shoulder.

"God Damn, that was a pretty good analogy, I think I can use that for my trials in the future, do you mind?" Max asked.

"Actually, you can use it with any profession in the place of the press. An attorney would fit nicely," Brad said as Wally laughed.

"OK here we go. Let' slap ol' Max with lawyers jokes." Max said as they walked into his office and sat around the huge conference table.

"Wally, tell me about John Doe." Brad asked with a stone serious face.

Wally spent the next two hours talking about the funerals that led up to John Doe. He described each time he made contact with the deceased and what he experienced. Brad did not show any signs of emotion, he just listened. Brad did not want to hear about John Doe just yet. He wanted Wally to repeat his contact with the others over and over. Wally then told Brad every detail that he could remember about John Doe. Brad listened quietly to every work with no emotions on his face.

"I think I have told you everything about my experiences and about John Doe." Wally said.

"Wally, I have been listening to you for over two hours. Do not be offended, but I have been hoping for some sort of inconsistency in your testimony to me. I guess I have dealt with too many politicians. They are great story tellers that are even better at lying. I can spot a liar a mile away. It is my joy to believe and trust my clients, as I told you this morning when we met. Max sent me your deposition. I hope you're not upset or think that I did not believe you. I have all the information I need. Let's prepare our statement for the cockroaches. I mean the press," Brad said with a reassuring smile.

Wally was fine with Brad's tactics. He had not lied nor did he have any reason to lie. He just wanted his life back to normal.

"Thank-you Wally, I have what I need. I will see you here at 5:30 p.m. sharp to get ready for the show." Brad said.

"Is that all you need" Do you want me to be familiar with what you are going to say?" Wally asked as he knew his fate would be in Brad's hands in front of all those microphones.

"Relax Wally, everything will be fine. I assure you of that. You better get some rest at home. We have a big evening and an even bigger tomorrow ahead." Brad said.

"Wally can go back to my home with his family. Wouldn't that be safer?" Max asked.

"No, Wally will be more comfortable in his own home with his family. Just pull down the shades, transfer your phones and sit back and enjoy your family. Why don't you run Wally home, Max?" Brad said.

"Sure, let's go out the back door." Max said as they grabbed their coats and left.

Brad sat at his laptop computer and started to prepare. As Brad was punching away at the keys, he was smiling. Wally was a very special person who wanted to have a normal life.

At 5:30 p.m., the press was lined up in front of Max's office and down the street. A podium from the high school was placed on the sidewalk with several microphones taped to it for all the networks that were there. This was a very big story with very little information for the press to go on.

The town marshal, county deputies and state police were on hand in case of a problem. The downtown was lined up with residents and outsiders who were curious about all of the publicity. The town of Goodland could be debt free if they could sell tickets to this press conference.

Max went to the funeral home to get his friend, Wally.

"How are you doing, little buddy?" Max said with a warm smile.

"I'm nervous. Do I have to be there? Brad is doing all of the talking, right? Wally asked.

"Yes, Brad is…and he needs you there. He showed me the outline of the briefing and you will be very happy with his work. Let's go to my office and get this show on the road." Max said as they drove to the office.

They entered from the back and gathered in the conference room.

"We have seven minutes and I am confident that this will clear your name and…" Brad was saying when Wally sharply interrupted.

"Do you think I can have my life back and get back to normal?"

"Wally, I am afraid that normal will be impossible, at least for awhile. Just hang in there. It will be fine. Now let me disinfect this virus," Brad said as he took out his leather bound notepad and walked out to face the crowd. Max and Wally followed like ducks in a row.

Bradley stood at the podium at exactly on time. Wally stood at his left and Max on his right.

"Thank-you for your patience. I am Bradley Funk and I will be briefing you on Mr. Wally Touch's relationship with, first Ross Salvitor; and second, the Barber murders. Let me preface that Mr. Touch is a funeral director, a loving husband and father. He is outstanding in his profession, a leader in the funeral industry. He is truly a care giver." He said turning to Wally with a smile.

"When someone that is loved dies, Wally is there for the family, doing everything in his power to lessen that families grief and giving them comfort. My father died last year and I wish that I would have known Wally and had him conduct his funeral. My family's hearts would have healed quicker if I had known of the genuine care that Wally gives. Many of you that live here in Goodland know that already.

"Let's talk about the Barber murders. Wally hadn't heard about the murders when they were reported by the media in the late eighties. No, Wally is not a suspect in the Barber murders.

"Wally was introduced to Mr. Salvitor, not years ago or months ago. He was first introduced to Mr. Ross Salvitor at the morgue, three days ago. Mr. Salvitor had been dead approximately five days. Mr. Wally Touch is not a suspect in the death of Mr. Salvitor. He was just a 'John Doe' to Wally Touch.

"Now because of Wally's caring nature and the time and respect that he gave to the families that he served; Wally developed a gift. He has the gift of 'touch'. When Wally makes contact with the deceased, he can somehow envision the lives that they lived as if he were there. If anyone has been to any of Wally's funeral services, they have understood, because Wally gave back this gift to the families he served. He did not care if it is a service attended by 500 family and friends or one single person with no one to grieve. Wally gives 150 percent to everyone he serves.

"Mr. Touch's gift led the Indiana State Police to an address that solved one of the most sought after serial killers of our time. Without Mr. Touch's gift, Mr. Salvitor would have been another John Doe buried in an unmarked grave.

"When the Chicago police came to gain information From Wally, they handcuffed him and dragged him to the Cook County jail. The District Attorney wanted a conviction for a crime that Wally did not commit. What crimes, you ask? It doesn't matter; Wally was a scapegoat…a feather in the District Attorney's cap.

"Will Wally's life ever be the same? I think not. Could Wally have said not a word about John Doe? I think so. Did Wally feel the need to tell of this heinous crime? Yes, he did!" Brad said as he patted Wally on the shoulder.

"My friend Wally is a good man and certainly a moral man. He has committed no crime, he only helped to reveal information that solved the Barber murders. Wally is here in Goodland to serve our families. Let's not forget that. Please do not judge him unfairly. Thank-you." Brad said as the press fired off questions.

Brad, Wally and Max stepped away from the podium after Brad finished answering questions. His answers seemed to satisfy the reporters and the crowd that had gathered. They went into Max's law office.

"Great job, Brad, you really know how to work a crowd," Max exclaimed as he gently slapped Brad on the back.

"Our flight leaves in 2 hours. Wally, for tomorrow, wear a dark navy suit, white button-down shirt and a wine tie. Never mind about the tie. I will bring you one. Appearance is everything on TV," Brad said.

"Lets meet at the airport in one hour boys," Max said.

"Are you going with us Max?" Wally asked.

"Damn straight I am. I've got to meet that Meredith Vieira, she is a hottie. It's not everyday your client is on the Today Show. Why, don't you want me to go?" Max asked.

"Sure I do, I just thought you would be too busy," Wally said.

"Hey, New York is a big city. I don't want my best friend to get lost or in any trouble. I'll be your body guard." Max said with a manly grin.

They met at the airport and boarded the NBC Citation Jet for LaGuardia Airport.

"The flight will take about two hours. This will give us time to go over your script," Brad said to Wally.

"Will the Chicago District Attorney be there?" Wally asked.

"He will not be at the New York studio, but he will be live via satellite at a Chicago studio. He will not be on your side, just remember that. There will also be a nationally renowned grief psychologist from Seattle Washington. His name is Allen McCray. I spoke with him on the phone and he is anxious to meet you. He believes in you. He doesn't understand what you have experienced, but he has documented similar stories in a few other funeral directors." Brad said.

"When did you talk to him and how did you find him?" Wally asked.

"Wally, just sit back and enjoy this ride. Research is my thing. Listen carefully. Some will think you are evil, that this is some form of demonic power. Some will think that you the second coming of Christ. Others will just think you are a flake or quack. I am just going to make you out to be a hero for solving the Barber Murders." Brad said.

"I have worked so hard to build trust and respect with families that I have served. I received a golden opportunity from Mr. William DeVere to own, not only a beautiful facility, but a funeral home with a flawless reputation, as when Mr. DeVere owned it. I want my old life back… will that ever be possible Brad? Wally asked as tears flowed from his cheeks.

"Wally, Max called me because his friend was in trouble. He knew that the press would have a field day with this. He even thought this could have gotten twisted and you could be blamed in some sick way and convicted.

I am going to get thing as normal as possible. Will they be the same? No. Will they be better, let's hope so." Brad said with a reassuring smile.

"Ma'am can I light this cigar?" Max asked the flight attendant as Wally and Bradley shook their heads no.

"Sir, there is no smoking, would you like a cocktail?" She asked with a smile.

"I thought you would never ask. I'll have an Old Style and if you don't have that, just surprise me." Max said sucking on the unlit cigar.

She brought a beer for Max and Wally and a white wine for Bradley.

Brad had been on the Today show and knew the format. Wally would be interviewed, but Brad could step in if something got tricky. It would be fifteen minutes of fame for Wally.

The plane touched down in a little less than two hours. The sky was releasing a very wet snow that melted as soon as it hit the pavement. A limo was waiting for the three men as they stepped off the plane. It would take them to the Plaza Hotel.

"I have wanted to go to this new restaurant with what I have heard has the ultimate cigar lounge in the back." Max said asking the driver if he had heard of such a place.

"No, sir, I am not familiar with it, but I'm sure you can get the name and address at the hotel desk. I'm sorry," the limo driver said.

"Wally, do you want to hit some nudie bars tonight?" Max asked with a laugh.

"I think not, Mr. Pervert. You can go alone if you want," Wally said as Brad quickly shouted.

"Don't even ask!!!!!!!!!'

"I was just kidding, besides we can probably use a good night sleep." Max said with a serious face.

They checked in at The Waldorf Astoria and Brad wanted to meet in one hour for dinner. Wally was impressed with his suite. NBC had a beautiful fruit and cheese basket with a note that read, 'compliments of NBC enjoy the Big Apple!'

Wally unpacked his garment bag, sat on the floral sofa and placed a call to Helen.

"Hi, Sweetheart, we just checked into the hotel. I am very nervous, but Max has a way of making me forget about the stress. You know how off the wall he is. I'm glad that he came. How are you holding up?" Wally asked.

"I'm glad that you are safe. The phone has been ringing ever since you left. A woman from West Virginia called and asked if you could father her child. Please tell me that everything will be alright." Helen said.

"What did you tell the lady from West Virginia?" Wally said with a chuckle.

"Oh you are a riot," she said. "You have been around Max too long."

"This Brad Funk has been on the Today show several times with politicians. He is not worried. How are the boys? Wally asked.

"They are fine, my mom and dad are here staying the night. You know how they love Grandma and Grandpa," Helen replied.

"Well, I have to clean up. We are meeting in the lobby for dinner. Max has his heart set on some restaurant that he wants to try. It has a cigar lounge; you know how he loves his cigars. I will call you when we get back. I love you Helen." Wally said in a love felt voice.

"You tell Max to behave. I love you more." Helen replied holding back tears.

Wally washed up and headed for the lobby. Max was already sitting on the couch, smoking a Cuban with his feet stretched out.

"Did you call Sweetie?" Max asked with a smile

"Yes I did and she wants you to try to behave yourself." Wally said as Max puffed away on his cigar.

The two men sat in the lobby, just people watching until Brad arrived.

"Well Brad is one-half hour late. He is probably glued to the phone. I'm going to light another cigar. Do you want one Wally?" Max asked as he pulled a Churchill out of his leather pouch.

"No thanks. For some reason a cigar does not sound good right now." Wally said shaking his head as Max tried to blow smoke rings.

Both Wally and Max watched Brad get off the elevator. Max was pointing at his watch. Brad came up to them smiling.

"Gentlemen, I have some great news, as well as some mildly bad news.

Dr. Allen McCray is joining us for dinner. He is excited to meet you, Wally. He has a grief and loss center in Seattle that helps all ages deal with the grieving process. He also has several books and videos on the subject as well. He agreed to come, because he felt that it would be good for the industry. He will be here in about twenty minutes. Max, please be on your best behavior. Dr. McCray is a kind, compassionate and wonderful human being. Keep the bad jokes and cheap cigars out of the conversation, please." Brad said.

"I'll have you know that this is not a cheap cigar. They're forty-five bucks a piece. For you and only you Brad, I will behave." Max said with a coy smile.

"Hey, what's the bad news, Brad?" Wally sharply said

"Well I have found out through a source that the Chicago police are working around the clock investigating you. They are trying to make you look like a fraud. If you have any skeletons in the closet, 'fess up', because they will find them," Brad said.

"Wally doesn't have any skeletons in the closet, but he does have a few in the basement…get it?" Max said with a loud laugh.

"That's what I do not want to hear, funeral humor." Brad snapped.

As the three men were talking, off the elevator walked a small man dressed in a polo button-down shirt, covered with a sweater vest, khakis and loafers. He had a raincoat draped over his arm, and was carrying a briefcase.

"Are you Bradley Funk?" the man asked in a kind yet humble voice.

"Yes, I'm Brad, Dr. McCray. This is Wally Touch and Max Goldburg." Brad said as he shook Dr. McCrays' hand.

"Please call me Allen. So you're Wally. I've heard so much about you from conversations with Brad and the NBC staff. It's a pleasure to meet you," Allen said as he shook Wally's hand.

"I'm pleased to meet with you; I have read several of your books. Your work is wonderful and so needed." Wally said with a smile.

"I was here on a conference, so this interview was convenient for me." He said.

"Shall we decide on a restaurant? We could always dine here?" Wally questioned. Max was disappointed because he knew the Hotel Restaurants are smoke free.

"I hear they have wonderful food at this hotel. That way we don't have to deal with taxis." Allen said.

The men walked into the restaurant, put their names on a list and went to the cocktail lounge. A waitress took their drink order.

"Wally, I would like to hear about your experiences. At my center, I deal with so much pain and sorrow; even joy after a loved one has died after a great deal of suffering. Your gift has been felt by not only funeral directors, but also family members.

Wally described in detail his experiences. Allen listened, nodding his head with acceptance. He absorbed every word that Wally so compassionately spoke. When Wally talked of Ross Salvitor, Allen felt sorry for what Wally was put through by the Chicago police Department.

"Wally it is so easy for people to be afraid of what they cannot explain or understand. Tomorrow on the Today Show, you will be questioned and judged. Some people will admire you, others will mock you. I have been criticized about sharing meaningful and fond memories of a lost love. I believe in the celebration of a life lived and holding it in our memories and sharing that love with our future generations to come. Many feel that when death has occurred; just have a service, bury your loved one and get on with your life. Let the person go. I believe just the opposite." Allen shared.

Wally and Allen did most of the conversing throughout dinner and desert.

"Gentleman, I have enjoyed this evening very much. I have some work to catch up on." Allen said as he shook hands and left the restaurant and hotel.

"What a great guy and I'm proud of you Max. No rude jokes or foul language. Are you changing, being around all of these good people?" Wally asked seriously.

No, I'm still my miserable self. The night is young. Let's all go to that cigar lounge." Max said.

Brad bowed out to get some work done. They need to be at the studio at 5:00 am. Brad suggested breakfast at 4:00 am and for Max and Wally to be in at a reasonable hour. Wally and Max hailed a cab for Max's smoker's delight.

CHAPTER 12

Wally, Allen, Max and Brad all had breakfast together the next morning. Brad gave some last minute instructions to Wally as well as Allen.

"Remember, we only have ten minutes to tell your story to have the truth prevail!" Brad said

A limo was waiting in front of the Plaza Hotel and the men were taken to the NBC studio. Wally and Allen were directed to makeup and then to the Green Room to wait for their appearance.

"I thought that you would be with us, Brad." Wally said.

"Well because of the time factor, they just want you and Allen. It will be fine, just tell your story." Brad said making Wally feel at ease.

"Oh by the way, NBC will not have the District Attorney on after all. That should make you shine." Brad then said with a smile

"You're on in five minutes," a producer cam in the Green Room and announced.

Wally took a deep breath and said, "I have butterflies in my stomach."

"Just treat the interview as if you are meeting a family for the first time." Allen said.

Wally and Allen were ushered out and seated during a commercial. Wally was white with fear until Meredith Vieira smiled and said;

"Relax, this isn't a dentist's office. You will do fine."

"I have with me Mr. Wally Touch, who is a funeral director in a small town in the Midwest and Dr. Allen McCray, who runs the Greif and Loss Center in Seattle, Washington. Good Morning Gentleman.

Wally, you solved one of the most puzzling unsolved murders of the century. You identified Ross Salvitor as the Barber murderer.

Could you tell us what happened leading up to the identification?" Meredith asked.

"Yes, thank-you, Meredith, as you said, I am a funeral director in a very small community in Indiana.

My wife and I purchased the DeVere Funeral home from William DeVere last year. I have always been motivated to be a care-giver, to help people who are hurting from the loss of a loved one.

I had a death call where I had to go to a home and make a removal; take the body out of the home. After the family had all said their goodbyes, I entered the bedroom alone. I noticed how peaceful the woman looked, as if she were soundly asleep. She was in her nineties and had lived a wonderful life. This may sound odd, but I touched her hand and I felt a warmth and goodness reach for my heart. I could see her past life as if I were there…her childhood, as a young woman with her new husband.

"The details and colors were vivid. I remember the smell of fresh baked bread. After the removal, I took her to my care to my funeral home. I told my wife and she suggested that we bake some bread that would fill the funeral home with the rich baked aroma.

When the family arrived to make the arrangement, they noticed the essence of freshly baked bread. They said that every Sunday, their mother would bake fresh bread. It brought tears to their eyes and to ours." Wally said as Meredith was moved by his words.

"Dr. McCray, with your devotion to aftercare and people coming to you for help with the loss of a loved one, how do you react to Wally?" Meredith asked.

"Thank-you, Meredith, I had the privilege of meeting Wally last night at dinner. He is a loving and caring man and I was inspired by his experience. Wally used what he envisioned to help those families get through the hardest times in their lives, the loss of a loved one. We can all sense happiness, danger, fear or love. Wally has a gift, the gift of touch." Allen said as he smiled at his new friend, Wally.

Helen, Teresa and Rev. Bob were all in front of the TV back in Indiana Watching Wally.

"Isn't he handsome? He even looks calm, but I know he is nervous," Helen said wiping tears of joy away. Every TV set in Goodland was locked on Channel 5; watching their local funeral director speak from the heart on national television.

"Tell us, Wally, about the Barber murders," Meredith asked?

"Prior to this, all of my contact has been with families that I knew. The coroner phoned me and told me of a John Doe found in a field, I was told if and not identified, I would have his funeral at the expense of the county. I went with the coroner to the morgue and on the way I kept wondering if I would feel anything when I touched John Doe's arm. When I went down to the basement and into the morgue, I was skeptical. I touched his forearm and felt a coldness and darkness, an evil feeling the likes of nothing I have ever experienced.

I saw a man take a woman's life as if it were of no consequence. I saw it so clear and I watched this man walk down a street ant into an intersection that I recognized…Michigan Avenue and Chestnut.

The man then walked north on Chestnut and into a building. I saw the address on the building. I was scared and in disbelief. I contacted my best friend, who is a local attorney, Max Goldburg and told him about what I experienced when I was at the morgue. He contacted a police investigator to check it out. The police investigator found out that the man was the Barber murderer." Wally confronted.

"We're about out of time. Dr. McCray, could you share your thoughts?" asked Meredith.

"Yes Wally should not be labeled as a so-called crime solver, but as a caregiver. Wally goes far beyond the typical funeral director role and into the hearts of the families he serves. Most people do not realize the demands of a funeral director. From the time they are called, to the time their loved one is at the cemetery or crematory there is much preparation. All funeral directors play such an important role in the ceremony of the death of a loved one. My friend Wally can not understand what all the fuss is about. He was just doing a job that the Lord put him here to do." Allen said.

"Thank-you, Mr. Touch and Dr. McCray. You have inspired me, I'm sure our listeners feel the same way." Meredith said before they went to commercial. She hugged Wally with tears of joy. Wally was then joined by Brad and Max.

"Great job, Wally, well done, you are a real TV pro now." Brad said.

"I think I am going to be sick," Wally said.

Wally's phone at home was ringing off the hook. The phone call that meant the most to Helen was from the Smithe family. They were very sorry for removing their father and using another funeral home. Many calls were to get Wally on a talk show and for interviews, even a book and movie deal.

The call that did however, bother Helen was from a man in Wisconsin. He told her that his wife had just passed away and he asked if Wally could touch her to see it she had been faithful to him. He told Helen that he would pay $25,000 for Wally's time.

Helen answered his request with a 'no'. After that call, she had the phones transferred to the answering service.

The men left the NBC studio with a feeling of joy and relief.

"Wally, please come to my clinic in Seattle soon. I enjoyed this experience. If you ever need anything, please don't hesitate to call me. I will go on any program with you if you feel I am needed." Allen said as he stepped into a cab.

Wally, Max and Brad were taken to the airport in NBC's limousine. Once in the limo, Max called his office for messages.

"Are you working or having a God-damn party while I am away?' Max asked his secretary.

"The phone has been ringing off the hook. The Illinois District Attorney said that he watched the Today show and for you to call him right away. Also you have a settlement offer for the Beck injury."

"Screw the Beck case… give me the number for the DA." Max said as she gave him the number. When Max hung up his secretary just smiled. She knew his bark was worse than his bite. Max is just a big teddy bear, trying to act harsh.

Max dialed the number.

"District Attorney's office, may I help you?" A receptionist asked.

"Get me Bob, please, this is Max Goldburg." Max said sternly.

"He is in a meeting, but he asked to be interrupted if you called. One moment please."

"Max, how are you? Say, we saw your program. I am going to make a statement to the press that Wally is not linked or investigated in anyway for the Barber murders or Ross Salvitor. We are sorry for putting Mr. Touch through this ordeal. Wally is a hero." Bob said.

"Bob, cut the shit, this is not like you to kiss ass. What do you think I am going to do about your department's misconduct with my client?" Max said in a controlled rage.

"Max, off the record, Gaglio was so out of line on this one. We wanted a conviction and I thought he brought me the murderer. Gaglio will also make a statement and he will be reprimanded." Bob said.

"Don't worry sport. We probably won't sue for much. But thanks for the information," Max said as he smiled at Wally in the limo.

"You're now a hero, my caring friend. The mayor will probably want to give you a key to the city of Chicago. But don't forget, three days ago they could have put you on the street and set fire to you and no one would have pissed on you to put you out. What a strange world we live in." Max said.

"Look I want to forget about my stay at the Cook County Jail. That's a chapter in my life that I want to forget. I really don't want to sue, OK? Wally asked.

"Wally, let me do what's best for you. I will discuss everything before I take any action, fair." Max said.

"I vote to sue the bastards!" Brad said.

The three men boarded the NBC charter for home. Brad had never worked with a client quite like Wally. His previous clients were no-name politicians with deep pockets or shady politicians that wanted to get re-elected. Brad did feel that Wally would be bombarded by people who wanted to use him for their own selfish reasons.

The plane ride was longer because they were unable to cruise at the same altitude as the previous day. All three men did not have much to say on the ride back except small talk, but they were all thinking about what the future had in store for Wally.

"I have a lot of catching up to do in my office. I hope tomorrow will be half-way normal." Max said.

"I did enjoy this Wally. If you ever need me, call. We just need to let the dust settle and evaluate. Your famous now, Wally," Brad said with a smile.

"I want to thank you both. I know this could have turned our very badly and I would still be sitting in jail. I'm glad you both stepped in on my side." Wally said

"Wait till he gets the bill and we see how happy he is with us," Max said as they all laughed. Max would not dream of billing his best friend a dime. He was one person that you wanted for you and not against you.

Brad was not interested in the money either. He loved helping Max and his friend, Wally. He had already several messages from people that wanted his services, after his affiliation with Wally.

Helen and Teresa were waiting at the municipal airport for the men. As the plane came into sight, Teresa looked at Helen and said, "Do you think this private jet will go to their heads?"

Helen just smiled and nodded her head. She ran up to Wally and gave him a big hug and kisses and did not want to let go.

"I missed you, Wally…you looked so sexy on TV." She said.

Max hugged his wife and said, "Yea, they keep mistaking me for Al Pacino. I had to beat the women off with a club. Honey, we have to get one of these toys," he said pointing to the Citation jet.

They all piled into the Suburban and took Max and Teresa home. Brad's care was already at Max's.

"Again, Wally, it was a pleasure and honor to be a part of your story." Brad said as he got into his car and drove off.

The other four exchanged hugs and Wally and Helen got back into their Suburban.

"Come on, Mr. Pacino and have your way with me." Teresa said as Max chased her into the house.

Wally could not wait to get home and see his boys. As they approached the drive, Wally saw many news vans still camped out in front of his funeral home. They pulled into the garage and disappeared as the door closed behind them.

As Wally lowered the door, he could hear the boys yelling, "Dad's home! Dad's home!"

They ran to greet him as he stepped out of the Suburban. Wally dropped to one knee as the boys embraced their dad. Helen came around to join them.

"Dad, you were real cool on TV," Sammy said.

"Jeremy, what happened to your eye? Come closer in the light so I can see." Wally said

"Oh, it's nothing Dad." Jeremy said with his head down.

"It looks like something to me, young man. Tell me what happened?" Wally asked.

"Well, one of the guys at school called you a murderer and said that you would get the gas chamber. Then at gym class, he said you were a psycho -killer. I told him at least my dad is not an unemployed drunk and then he hit me." Jeremy said.

"So, what did you do? Did your teacher step in? Who was this boy?" Wally asked.

"He waited until we were all walking into the dressing room. The teachers were in their offices. So I punched him in the face and threw him to the ground. The teacher ran in and pulled me off of him. We both said we were playing around to avoid going to the principal's office. I did get the best of him," Jeremy said as he puffed his chest.

"Who was this kid?" Wally asked.

"It was Haskell Dieter," Jeremy answered

"You could right. His dad does to have more problems when he drinks. Did you put him down with a right or left?" Wally asked as he shadow boxed the wall.

"Wally, you know I don't approve of fighting, but he did seem to deserve it," Helen said as the family all laughed.

"No more fighting, young man, promise me! You are lucky that you didn't get suspended." Helen said in a stern voice.

"I promise Mom." Jeremy said

"Come on Rocky, let's go in the living room and watch pro-wrestling." Wally said as he put Sammy on his back.

"Always jokes around here," Helen said as she followed the three most important men in her life.

Dinner that night was simple. Pizza delivered by a local parlor called Grubs. They have the best Sicilian pizza in Northern Indiana. They boys loved pizza nights. After dinner, Wally and Helen sat on the couch and the boys were on the carpet watching TV.

"This is my favorite time in the whole world, just watching our boys in front of us, healthy and happy, makes me realize what a miracles they are. I love you, Helen." Wally whispered as he kissed his loving wife tenderly.

That night Wally really did not care what was on television. He was just happy to be with his beloved family. That night Wally curled up in his own bed next to Helen. He slept like a baby.

CHAPTER 13

The next morning, Wally got up early to fix a big breakfast. It was 6:30 am, and he had to wait until 7:00a.m. for the local grocery to open to get milk. He set the table and got everything ready as his family slept.

He was dressed in Levi's, flannel shirt and Docksiders with a polo baseball cam to hide his unruly hair. Wally put on his coat and headed for the grocery.

He put some loose change into the machine to get a Sunday paper and waited in his Suburban until the grocery opened. As Wally started to read the front page, he looked up as he heard tapping on the glass. Wally rolled down the window.

"Wally are you OK? We were sick when we found out that you had murdered a bunch of people. Heck our boys have been to your house before, to play with yours. Then we saw you on TV. Wally, my husband and I were sure glad that you didn't murder anybody. Wally, can you tell me how long I have to live?" the lady asked as she grabbed Wally's hand and would not let go.

"Please, don't do that ma'am," Wally said as he jerked his hand away,

"I am not a fortune teller. Good day," Wally said as he rolled up his window and tried to keep his anger to himself. The woman just stood there in shock and then walked away.

Wally went into the grocery store at just after seven in the morning. All eyes were on him and he could tell that some people did not know how to treat Wally.

"Hello, Mr. Murfitt," Wally said to the owner of the grocery store. "How are you?

"Oh, I'm fine, Wally, how are you? I saw you on TV." Mr. Murfitt said shyly, looking away.

Wally went to the refrigerated section where the milk was kept. He grabbed a gallon of milk and checked out. No one said a word. Wally checked his skin to see if he might have developed leprosy.

He returned home and started to prepare his big breakfast for his sleeping family. As Wally started cooking, his beeper went off. It was the answering service.

"Good morning, this is Wally at DeVere Funeral Home. You beeped me?" Wally asked.

"Yes, Wally, we have seventy-one messages for you. Most of them are from Newspapers and TV stations. You have five death calls," she said as Wally panicked.

"What? Five calls! Why didn't you beep me sooner?" Wally said sharply.

"All of the calls are out of state but one. They all know about your power and want to know if you will travel to do their services. One is in Hawaii.

The last call was the nursing home. Mrs. Sullivan just passed away." She said.

"I am terribly sorry that I jumped at you. Things are very hectic around here. Thank-you," Wally said to the woman on the phone.

"That's OK. From listening to you on TV, Mr. Touch, I sure wish you could have had my grandmother's funeral. Not so much for your gift, but for your loving compassion. It seemed like the funeral director that conducted the service did not care about my grandma." She said.

"Well, thank-you. Could you please e-mail all of my messages to me, please? Wally asked.

He called the nursing home and told them that he would be right over. Mrs. Sullivan was 105 years old. She died peacefully in her sleep.

Wally finished making breakfast for his family. The boys were already at the table still in their pajamas, ready to dig in. Wally prepared a plate for Helen and took it to her in bed. The smell of the sausage woke her up.

"Oh, honey, how sweet. I was going to get up and make you breakfast." She said fighting to wake up and wiping the sleep out of her eyes.

"I have to go to the nursing home. The boys are already eating. If all goes well, I can get Mrs. Sullivan ready and still make the 10:00a.m. church service." Wally said as he kissed Helen on her forehead. Wally quickly showered and put on the proper coat and tie. He patted the boys on their heads, grabbed a sausage patty as he left the house.

When he drove up to the nursing home, he was shocked at all the news trucks. This was unacceptable and inappropriate. He parked in the back and was swarmed with camera and questions.

"Can we film you when you touch the woman's hand? Will you tell us what her life was like?" a reporter asked.

"It's not 'a woman'! It's Mrs. Irene Sullivan, who was 101 years old and has lived her all here life. You have me in a very awkward position here. My job is to take her in my care and I will not allow any of you to disturb her. No, you cannot film her or be in the room. Please back off so I can do my job here!" Wally said as he removed the cot from the hearse and entered through the back door.

Wally was greeted by a familiar nurse. "Oh hi, Wally. Someone from here tipped off the press. I would love to get my hands on them. Mrs. Sullivan is down the hall in room twenty-seven. I will take you there. I saw you on TV. You were great. I always knew you were special." She said as they went into Mrs. Sullivan's room.

"Could you keep the press out, please? I cannot believe how cold they can be under these circumstances," Wally said.

"You bet, I will stand in front of the door. Let them try to get past me," the nurse said with a grimacing face.

Wally stood over this frail old woman with long sterling grey braided hair pulled to one side.

She was in a nightgown buttoned to the neck with a housecoat over the nightgown. Wally looked at her and smiled. He did not have to see the life she had lived to know that she was a kind and sweet person. Her peaceful appearance told him that.

Wally placed his hand on her hand and closed his eyes. He felt the warmth of her life fill his heart. Wally saw a large stone house on a sprawling hill that bordered a peaceful creek and the property had the most ornate iron fence that Wally had ever seen.

In this huge home was a large dining room with a mahogany table. On the table was a turkey with all the trimmings. Everyone around the table was bowing their heads in prayer.

There were thirteen children with the father at the head of the table. Everyone was elegantly dressed for what appeared to be a festive occasion. Wally smiled when he saw a little girl, no more than twelve years old, with long blonde hair braided to one side. The room smelled of turkey and pumpkin pie.

A knock at the door brought the father up and out of his chair. At the door was a woman in rags holding a child? The father quickly took the child into the study and grabbed his black bag. This small child was blue and not breathing. The father removed a chicken bone that was lodged in the child's throat. The woman wept with joy as the child's color returned to normal.

Before the woman left, the father prepared a meal for her to take home. The woman did not want to accept their generosity. After much persuasion from the father, she gratefully received their gift.

Wally then saw a woman standing in front of a large building in a metropolitan city, presenting a check for the homeless. Wally could see her blue eyes shine with love. Her long blonde hair was pulled to one side in a braid. She was wearing a silk dress. Wally saw the nurse that was outside the door bringing tea to Mrs. Sullivan as she did everyday at three in the afternoon. She sat at her bedside and listened to the wonderful stories of Mrs. Sullivan's incredible life. Wally then opened his eyes when he heard a knock at the door.

I'm Irene Sullivan's granddaughter. May I come in?" She asked as Wally opened the door.

"I just got here from Connecticut. I am so mad at myself for not being here when she died." She said in tears.

"Your grandmother was an extraordinary woman. She has such long and beautiful hair.' Wally said.

"She always wore it long, braided and to one side." She said with a smile.

"Was her father a physician?" Wally asked.

"Why yes he was. He was such a great man. Grandma always told us stories about him. I am sorry that I interrupted you. I just wanted to see her. I'll go so you can finish." She said.

"I would be happy to leave the room, if you would like to spend some time with your grandmother." Wally said with a smile.

"I would like that, thank-you," she said as Wally left the room.

He waited outside the room for about five minutes. The door opened and the young woman smiled as she wiped away the tears from her red face.

"Than-you for letting me be with her," she said as she hugged Wally.

"Not at all, I am so glad that you got here. Now I will take your grandmother into my care." Wally said as he went back into the room. Wally placed Mrs. Sullivan on the cot and wheeled her to the door for the last time. He saw the nurse sobbing.

"What's wrong?" Wally asked

"Oh, I'm going to Miss Irene so much," she answered.

"Are you curious if I saw anything when I touched Mrs. Sullivan?" Wally asked.

"Yes, but I wouldn't dare say anything. I know you have a job to do." She said.

"You know, Nurse Johnson, when I see the life lived of a person that I am taking into my care, it is usually the best part of their lives. I saw many wonderful things in Mrs. Sullivan's life. I saw you take tea to her at 3:00 p.m. every day. I saw you spending time with her. She did love your company." Wally said as he hugged the nurse.

"Oh, thank-you for telling me that. I will never forget her." She said whimpering as Wally opened the door to leave the nursing home.

Wally stepped outside and the mood quickly changed. There were reporters and cameramen surrounding his hearse.

"Did you have a vision, Wally? Tell us!" a reporter blurted out with many questions following.

Wally opened the hearse door and placed Mrs. Sullivan in very carefully. He shut the door and with all of the news microphones in his face and everyone waiting for him to speak.

He said, "Shame on all of you. If this were your mother or grandmother, how would you feel? You are very rude and disrespectful." He got into his hearse and drove to the funeral home.

Wally finished in the prep room with Mrs. Sullivan at 9:30a.m. He had time to clean up and take his family to church.

"Boys, are you ready?" It's time to go!" Wally yelled as his boys came down the stairs dressed in dark suits with conservative ties. Dressed like little undertakers. Wally smiled as they scampered down the stairs.

"You boys clean up pretty good," he said.

"Dad, I'm embarrassed about my eye. It got darker this morning," Jeremy said.

"Son, if someone says anything, just look them square in the eye and say…'you should see the other guy'," Wally said with a wink.

Helen has on a dress that is one of Wally's favorites. "Oh what a vision of loveliness. Honey, you look wonderful," "I guess this means that we are eating out." Wally said smiling at Helen as she graced the stairway.

They loaded into the Cadillac and arrived as the church bells were ringing.

Seating in a small town church is like owning your own pew. Some families have been sitting in the same pew for six generations. Wally's pew was near the back center part of the church.

As Wally and his family walked in, everyone in the church stood up to sing the first hymn. They easily got to their seats, picked up a hymnal and began to sing with the congregation. Wally and Helen could feel the eyes upon them. People were curious.

When the song concluded, Rev. Bob put both hands in the air as the congregation was seated.

"Glorious day that the Lord has given us. I want to welcome you all. Are there any visitors here today?" Rev. Bob said as he looked around the church

He did, however, see a group of people with cameras standing in the back of the church. He did not acknowledge their presence.

Rev. Bob continued, "I would like to take a moment to welcome Wally back. I keep hearing about Wally's gift. I cannot believe that they are just now finding that out.

"Wally has had a gift ever since he started serving our families. I have known Wally for a long time and his gift is merely him being himself.

"I have a confession to make to all of the members, press and reporters that are here today. I, too have a gift. I have had my gift for thirty-seven years, when I took my first church. Father Riley, at the Catholic Church, has had his gift much longer than I. When I visit a shut-in who is depressed about growing old or not being about to get around anymore, I use my gift to try and help their hearts heal. When I visit a hospital, I try to do the same.

"I recall visiting a woman several years ago in the hospital before she passed away. I watched her sleep so peacefully, I placed my hand on hers and she opened her eyes and smiled. I said nothing to her. I just watched her and I could feel in my heart that she felt safe. As I moved my hand, her eyes got big and she grabbed my hand and held on so tightly. I sat there and just held that sweet tiny hand until she fell asleep.

"On my drive home, I thought about what had happened at the hospital. All she wanted was to be touched and loved. She died shortly after that and I will never forget the peace in her eyes as we held hands.

"You see, I have it very easy. I touch the hearts, hands and souls of the living. Wally, however, touches the lives of those touched by the angel of death and their families. He does not have it so easy, but yet Wally makes it seem so easy and natural.

"I have attended several of Wally's funeral services at both the DeVere Funeral Home and Chester Funeral Home. On certain occasions I heard families wish that Wally could have conducted their relative's funerals. The families told Wally this, because of the care he gives every family he touched. The reason I speak of this today is because I am concerned about the media attention." Rev. Bob said as he stared to the back of the room at the reporters.

"Wally is my friend. He is a friend to the community. It would be a shame to drive him away, because he can not do his job effectively. Please give him the love and support and privacy he deserves. You have just heard half of my sermon early. Please stand and sing hymn number 423, Onward Christian Soldiers." Rev. Bob said as the congregation stood and began to sing.

Wally smiled at Rev. Bob. He knew that he said all that because he knew that Wally was hurting and tired of all the attention. He now had the support and respect of his church. Wally felt very comfortable with the rest of the service.

"Powerful sermon! Rev. Bob, Powerful!" Wally said after church as he shook Rev. Bob's hand on his way out.

"I did not notice you nodding off, which is a great sign," Bob said to his friend with a chuckle as they walked down the steps of the church.

"Wally, remember to call me anytime if you need me, OK?" Rev. Bob said as they walked out the door.

"Where do my troops want to eat?" Wally asked as they got into the Cadillac.

"You pick the place, honey. You have already put in a full day." Helen replied.

"Well, if I pick the place, I say we go to the Beef House. The arrangements are at 4:00 pm. that gives us plenty of time. How does that sound?" Wally asked as they all agreed.

The Beef House was a forty-five minute drive. They served great steaks and had a wonderful salad bar.

"Dad, did you have to put on make-up before you went on TV?" Sammy asked.

"Yep, they gave me a free haircut and my face got the works. Why do you ask?" Wally asked.

"I don't know. Was being on TV fun or were you scared?" Sammy again asked.

"Well, I was nervous. Boys, I never told you the reason that I went to jail. I know that your mother told you not to ask me about it. It all happened because I thought I was doing the right thing by having Max check out a Chicago address that I saw when I touched John Doe…which was Ross Salvitor." Wally said.

"I don't understand what you mean when you say you see something when you touch a dead person," Jeremy said.

"OK boys, close your eyes. You are both hungry, right?" Wally said as the boys nodded their heads 'yes'. Now think about what you are going to have to eat…a thick, juicy steak or deep fried chicken. Think real hard about the food that sounds good….do you see it?" Wally asked in a soft voice.

"I can see a plate with a big, juicy T-bone on it," Jeremy answered with delight.

"I can't see anything except the dark," Sammy said in disgust.

OK, close your eyes again, not too tight. When you clean your room without being told, what kind of ice cream does Mom get you at the grocery?" Wally said as Helen smiled.

"Chocolate, that's my favorite!" Sammy said excitedly.

Now, think about a big bowl of chocolate ice cream with a big scoop of whipped cream on top with melted chocolate running into the bottom of the bowl," Wally said

"I can see it, Dad. I really can see the bowl of ice cream. Sammy said.

"Well, that is what I see but, I see a person's past life. Most of the things I have seen were good things. The man that they found murdered over twenty-five woman in Chicago. Maybe God felt that the girl's families and the world deserved to know what really happened." Wally sighed.

For the rest of the drive, Wally told the boys details of the wonderful things that he experienced when he had taken the families loved ones under his care. He did not, however, give the boys detail about Ross Salvitor.

It was nice for Wally and his family to have lunch in peace. Not to be bothered by questions and camera.

"I have never seen a kid eat so much. Where do you put all that food? Do you have a hollow leg, Sammy?" Wally asked poking at Sammy's belly.

"No, dad, you know my leg is not hollow," Sammy said with a serious expression on his face. The whole family laughed. Wally paid for the bill and they all headed for home.

"Jeremy, I hope Dad won't be able to touch us and tell if we have been bad or something." Sammy said.

"Are you feeling a little guilty, I don't need to touch you to know that." Wally said with a heavy laugh.

The boys were giggling in the back seat. It was a good day for the Touch family.

Mrs. Sullivan's granddaughter was the only family member to show up for the funeral arrangement. She was the only one left in the Sullivan family.

She told Wally fabulous stories this 101 year old gem. Wally knew that this would be a rather small service, consisting of nursing home staff and a few residents and Mrs. Sullivan's granddaughter. The visitation and funeral would be held on the same day.

Wally was back to is old self, until he went through his e-mail messages. Many messages were from broadcasters that wanted Wally on their programs. There were three messages from the families of victims of the Barber murders. Also a few off the wall requests, like if Wally would bless this person's dog or if Wally was from another galaxy.

Wally did, however, want to return a message from a mother of one of the victims. The message stated that her daughter was the last person killed by Ross Salvitor. So Wally called Mrs. Kessler.

Hello, I am Wally Touch and I am returning your call." Wally said in a soft voice.

"Oh, thank-you so much for calling. We are grateful to you. Anne's death has been haunting us for years. We prayed every day that someone would be found responsible. The years went by and our hopes faded each day. Do you remember what the woman looked like and what she was wearing?" She asked.

"Mrs. Kessler, remember this was a vision or dream like state that I was in. It could have been any of the twenty-seven women." Wally said.

"Wally, did he take any articles of clothing off of her?" She again asked.

"No. he did not. He followed her at a distance down a side street alley. I do remember she was a beautiful young girl, with a sleeveless dress on and she also had a briefcase or a computer case with her." Wally said

"Was the case brown?" she asked sobbing on the phone.

"Why yes, that was our daughter. She was the only victim that still had her shoes on. Salvitor would always take his victim's shoes off before or after he took a lock of hair. Oh, my God, that was your sweet child. I am very sorry," Wally said as she wept on the phone.

"Did…did she suffer? I have to know." she said with hesitation.

"No, I don't think she suffered." Wally said thinking about the horrific way she died. Telling her details would be wrong.

"I do remember her beautiful smile. Again, I am so sorry for your loss." Wally said.

"I called the detectives to get any information. They said in the paper that they have several of Salvitor's diaries, but they will not give out any information.

Did you know that the bastard inherited forty million dollars? He had all the bills paid by computer, the money taken right out of his account. They would have never caught him. Thank-you for your time. You have been so helpful." Mrs. Kessler said.

"Mrs. Kessler, you should call or get books by Dr. Allen McCray. He can help you with your loss. Please take care of yourself." Wally said as he hung up the phone.

"Who were you talking to, Hon?" Helen asked.

"I got a message from one of the victim's mothers and I called her. I know it has not been long, but I bet the police could have let them read through the Salvitor diaries. They know by now why he killed. What a tragedy!

The families of these women finally know more about what happened and now possibly why it happened?

Maybe Max can help us get some answers," Wally said.

"Wally, this murder stuff is over. Please, our lives have changed enough as it is." Helen said as she went upstairs in tears.

Wally sat for a while to collect his thoughts, and then he went upstairs.

"You're right, dear. I know I should not have anything to do with the Barber Murders, but I feel that I am a link to the crimes. Let's lie down and take a nap and let me hold you tight?" Wally asked Helen as he gently kissed her soft lips.

CHAPTER 14

Mrs. Sullivan's funeral was attended by her granddaughter and a few staff members from the nursing home and local hospital. Wally had to be vocal at the gravesite and chase some of the press away. After the funeral, Wally sat at his desk to get caught up on some paperwork when the phone rang. Wally did not transfer the phone and was prepared for a prank call.

"Good Afternoon, DeVere Funeral Home, Wally speaking," Wally said in a monotone voice.

"Wally, how are you my friend, it's Allen. I got home last night and started writing about you and your experience. I have been writing all day and just had to call. Did you recover from the Big Apple?" Allen asked.

"It's good to hear from you, Allen. I can use some of your positive energy right now." Wally said.

"What's going on… can I help with anything?" Allen said with concern.

"No, its just TV stations, big newspapers and radio stations breathing down my throat. I did get a call from a mother of one of the victims of the Barber murders. I gave her your number. I think you can help her." Wally said

"Yes, Mrs. Kessler. She called me already. I am sending her two of my books. She seems like such a kind and gentle person, but has been haunted because of the tragedy in her life from the death of her daughter.

I will help her." He said.

"I just finished a service and at the grave site, it really started to get to me, I just want…" Wally said as Allen interrupted.

"Wally, I have been writing down thoughts that will help people who have lost a loved one. I am tuning in on the relationship between the funeral director and the deceased's family. I have always known that a funeral director plays a key roll in the funeral ritual and the healing process.

"Wally, you will play a deeper role, as if you are your part of the family and you are taking your own family member into your care." Allen said.

"I'm not sure what every other funeral director does and I know some excellent ones. I do, however, conduct a funeral from start to finish from the heart. That's how I always conducted my services." Wally said.

"I know the press is getting to you, Wally. Come to Seattle. Bring your wife and family. Come out for a few days. I want to show you what I do. It will be a mini-vacation for you. I'll send you tickets. What do you say?" Allen asked.

"Oh, you don't have to send tickets, Allen. I am so honored that you invited me. I would be delighted to bring my family to see you and your center in Seattle. In your book, I remember a quote that I use in my service; 'a funeral is a celebration of life for families and friends that pay their respects to a loved one lost'. Did I get it right? I have focused on that quote of yours, Allen and try to make my funeral services all memorable. Everyone deserves a great funeral." Wally said.

"I couldn't have said it better. The evening we met in New York, you said that you have read most of my books. I don't write books for people like you, Wally. You already have the concept; you've passed the test and received an A+. I write books for people who struggle with the loss of love or struggle because they did not say good-bye, or were mean or rude to the person before they died. They need me to help heal the pain and guilt inside.

"Wally, come out and see me. Who knows, you and Helen might not want to leave Seattle." Allen said.

"I will talk to Helen tonight and see you before spring. Thank-you, my friend." Wally said.

"Well get your calendar and get your tickets. Good talking with you, Wally. Remember, what they do not know about you, they will never understand. I wish you and your family the best," Allen said before he hung up.

Wally enjoyed hearing from Allen. He walked into the kitchen and poured a glass of grape juice. Out of the kitchen window, he saw Sammy talking to a reporter. Wally could see that Sammy was uncomfortable with the conversation that they were having. Sammy kept shaking his head 'no', and as Sammy walked away, the reporter kept following. That was all Wally could take.

Wally went outside and crossed the street and approached the reporter and Sammy.

"What is going on here, Mister? Leave my boy alone…are we clear?" Wally said as he got into the reporters face.

"Chill out, Mr. Touch. I was just asking your son some questions, that's all." The reporter said.

"What could you possible gain by talking to a nine year old boy? It's bad enough that you are camped out in front of my home, that you follow us to church; you even follow me to my removals. But you will not bother my son!" Wally shouted.

As soon as Sammy started to step into the street a Channel 13 news truck came roaring around the corner. Wally heard the truck, but the driver did not see Sammy because of all the news trucks around the funeral home blocking the truck's view.

As the truck turned at a fast speed, Sammy froze in terror and Wally ran and yelled, "No Sammy!"

Wally sprinted and pushed his son out of harm's way, just as the truck made contact will Wally.

The truck skidded to a stop, but it was too late. When the truck struck Wally, the impact threw him backwards and his head bounced against the pavement. Sammy ran to his dad, screaming. Someone yelled, "Call 911" and a group of newspaper reporters circled Wally and Sammy.

"Somebody help my Daddy, please!" Sammy cried out.

The ambulance is on the way, son," a cameraman said as he was filming.

The only sound heard was Sammy's sobs. As the blasts of the siren echoed through the streets, Helen looked outside and ran to the street.

"Oh, my God! Oh no! What happened Sammy?" She said as she dropped to her knees and held Wally's hand.

Wally opened his eyes and looked at Helen and Sammy and smiled.

"Are you OK, son? I could not go on without you" He turned and said to Helen. "Oh, hi, sweetheart. Have I told you how much I love and adore you? I just had the most beautiful dream. I was at my Grandma Touch's house for Thanksgiving. Our whole family was there. Grandma was in the kitchen cooking turkey and dressing, green beans, homemade rolls the melt in your mouth and pumpkin pie.

"Did I ever tell you how wonderful her pies were? Well, anyway, Grandpa was in the living room with great uncle Charlie. He was tapping his cane on the floor. They were watching TV. My mom and dad were sitting at the dining room table talking to my aunt and uncle. My brother was there, too. Did I tell you how much I miss him?" Wally said as the paramedics arrived and placed the body board next to him.

"Wally, are you OK, buddy? Where do you hurt?" The paramedic said

"I think I'm fine. I just can't get up or move my legs. My head does feel a little funny. Where's Sammy? Come here son." Wally said trying to force a smile.

The paramedics placed Wally on the body board and strapped him in. He noticed blood coming out of Wally's ear and looked at Helen. She saw the blood and she could see in the paramedic's eyes that Wally was hurt pretty bad.

"Mrs. Touch, you are welcome to ride with us to the hospital. Sammy will you run and get your brother?" The paramedic said.

Sammy ran into the house and found his brother playing a video game on the computer.

"Jer, come quick, its dad." Sammy said as they both ran out of the house and into the front of the ambulance.

The paramedic loaded Wally into the ambulance. Helen would not let go of Wally's hand. He fought to keep his eyes open. Helen lovingly looked into Wally's kind soft eyes, smiling at her husband.

"I'm a little dizzy, hon. I don't feel so good right now." Wally said as his eyes slowly closed.

"Oh my God, Wally, hang on, sweetie. We are almost there. Please, please hang on!" Helen said as his grip failed.

Helen closed her eyes and saw Wally in blue jeans, flannel shirt and cowboy boots. Oh, how he loved his cowboy boots. Wally was playing what appears to be hide and go seek in a large woods. He was counting to twenty-five with his head against a huge sycamore tree. Helen saw people running and laughing, trying to hide from Wally.

"Ready or not, here I come." Wally said as he turned. Helen could see his face glow with happiness. He saw a woman behind the tree and gave her a big hug.

"Mrs. DeVere, so good to see you. I did not know that you were playing. I thought you were my brother Ted. I thought only Ted and Justin were playing.

"No, Wally we are all here. We have been waiting for you," Mrs. DeVere said with a smile.

Wally looked over the clearing and saw twenty-seven women sitting at an oversized picnic table. They were laughing and singing.

"Hi Wally, come join us when you are done playing." They were all dressed in the most beautiful, bright floral dresses. Wally knew every girl's name.

"Is that you, Mrs. Miller…and Mr. Smithe… when did you both get here?" Wally asked.

They were sitting on a park bench overlooking a beautiful crystal blue lake with ducks and swans swimming on the surface.

Hello, Wally. We beat you here. Isn't this paradise?" Mrs. Miller asked as she pointed to the lovely landscape.

Wally turned as his brother, Ted and Justin ran for the base. Wally smiled and took off running after them. They were all laughing.

Ted slipped and fell and Wally stopped, his face filled with horror. Justin ran to Ted and started to tickle him and he turned over laughing.

Wally ran over and hugged Ted.

"I have missed you, Ted. There has not been a day that goes by that I did not think of you." Wally said as a tear rolled from his eye.

"I know little brother, I have watched down on you and I am so proud of you. We can be together now, here with all out family." Ted said as he pointed to a magnificent archway to a city more beautiful than anything that Wally had ever seen.

"Ted, did I die? Is this heaven?" Wally asked.

"Well, let's put it this way. You are reborn. Reborn into paradise and all you see is yours to explore. Everyone will look familiar, because we are all family here." Ted said.

As Wally walked into the city, he saw hundreds of people and he knew all of them.

"Dad, oh, my gosh! Is that really you?" Wally said to a man on a bench. He stood and embraced his son.

"Yes, son, your grandma and grandpa are inside waiting to see you." He said as he pointed to a beautiful cottage.

"Dad, I have so much to tell you. I've missed you so, Ted is here too," Wally said with great joy.

"Son I have missed you too and I see your brother every day. There will be plenty of time to catch up." He said with a smile.

"I have two fine sons dad, and my wife is so beautiful. I love her so. Wait, wait a minute! What about Helen…" Wally said as the image went dark.

"Helen! Helen! It's Dr. Amos, we need to get Wally to the emergency room," he said to her as she opened her eyes.

She looked down at Wally and the tears began to fall.

"It's too late" It's too late!" she said weeping.

The Doctor and staff got Wally out of the ambulance and Helen and the boys followed. They wheeled him into the trauma room. Helen and the boys went to the waiting room. She had a distant expression on her face as if she were lost and numb with disbelief. Max arrived soon after and found Helen and the boys.

"I just got the call. I am so sorry. It will be all right. Do they know anything yet?" Max asked trying to comfort Helen.

"He's gone, Max. What will I do?" She said and Max held her as they waited. Teresa arrived as did Helen's parents. They all sat in the room and waited.

'Three years ago, I took Wally's eel skin boots to the Goodwill Store," Helen said out of the blue. Everyone in the waiting room turned to listen.

"Wally bought the boots and a Stetson hat back during those Urban Cowboy days in the early 1980's. Every man wanted to be a cowboy. Wally called his boots his rootin' tootin', boogie boots. He looked ridiculous in those boots. But he loved them. He would tuck his jeans in the boots and pull his pants up above his belly button and do this stupid dance, clicking his heels with his thumbs tucked in the front pockets." Helen said with a smile. No one said a word; they just let Helen tell her story…

"Once in a great while, before I got rid of the boots, we would go out and they would end up on his stocking feet. He would dance around while I got ready. God, he looked like a dork when he tucked them in. I think at that moment, Wally thought he was a real cowboy."

"Shortly after I got rid of the boots we had planned to see a movie and go to dinner. He was in his closet and I could hear him going through all the boxes. He came into the living room and asked if I knew where his rootin' tootin' boogie boots were. He said that he felt lucky that night. I told him that I took some things to the Goodwill.

He had such a disappointed expression on his face, but he never got mad or yelled at me. He just said that it was OK. I suffered through dinner and the movie thinking about those stupid boots.

"The next morning, I went to Goodwill to see if I could buy back the boots. The boots were no where to be found. I asked the clerk for some help. She told me that items like Cowboy boots and leather jackets go quickly. I cried all the way the way home," Helen said.

Dr. Amos came into the waiting room and looked at Helen with heavy eyes. She knew that the news was going to be bad.

"Helen, Wally sustained some massive head injuries. We did all that we could for him. I'm sorry," he said shaking his head

Max quickly got up and looked at Dr. Amos and said, "No! No! This is unacceptable, get back in there and save my best friend's life, please!" He just dropped to his knees and wept over the loss of his best friend.

Dr. Amos again expressed his feelings of sorrow and went back into the emergency room. Helen and Teresa helped Max up and the boys came over and hugged their mom. Max and Teresa wrapped their arms around the Touch family and they stood in the middle of the room and cried. No one was allowed into that waiting room until they were ready to leave. Max and Teresa took Helen home and Helen's parents took the boys.

"Max, Wally always got things done around here, he paid all the bills. He kept our family going. I don't know what to do." She said in tears.

"Helen, several months ago, Wally was over drinking beer with me while I smoked a cigar. Out of the blue, he said, what would happen if I suddenly died? So we made arrangements for him as well as me. I have it on my laptop. Wally chooses his casket, vault, even his casket spray. He also picked the music to be played at visitation as well as the service. "Something in the Way She Moves, by James Taylor, was on the list." Max said.

He loved James Taylor, could you handle this for me. Please?" Helen asked as the tears started to roll down her cheeks.

"I sure will, dear. I will call Vince Bowen to handle the funeral. Wally had the utmost respect and admiration for him. Is that OK?" Max asked.

"Max, see if Mr. DeVere would handle the service. Please ask him, or see if he would just help with the service." She asked.

"I sure will," Max said as he hugged Helen.

"Do you want Max and me to stay with you and the boys," Teresa asked.

"Thank-you, but I want to be alone with the boys. I will call you if I need you." Helen said.

"I'll check on you in the morning, dear." She said.

Max and Teresa left the funeral home. Max was angry. He was upset with the media. He blamed the Chicago police and he was regretful that his best friend Wally got involved.

He went into his office at home, opened an Old Style and lit a cigar. He stared out the picture window.

"Max, can I sit in here with you?" Teresa asked.

Honey, you hate these cigars…here I will put it out." Max said as he reached for the ash tray.

"No, it doesn't bother me. Please don't put it out. I love you Max and I am so scared for Helen. Why did this have to happen to our friends?" Teresa said as she curled up on Max's lap and put her head on his shoulder. She felt so safe with her big teddy bear of a husband. Max took one puff and let the cigar go out as he held his wife.

The next morning, Max called Mr. DeVere and asked if he would perform the funeral ceremony for Wally. Mr. DeVere had heard of Wally's death the night before. He was saddened as well as shocked.

"Max, yes I would be honored to conduct his funeral. Wally was the finest young man that I have ever met. We can never choose when our time is up and it never seems fair. I lost my wife and now I feel as if I have lost a son. Please tell Helen that I will handle everything. I will have Vince Bowen make the removal at the hospital. He is a fine man as well," Mr. DeVere said.

"I think Wally has pretty much made his own arrangement. Would you like for me to bring over what he had planned?" Max asked.

"Why does it not surprise me that Wally took care of himself, so that no one would be burdened? When Mrs. DeVere died, Wally knew I was in no shape to make rational decisions. Wally sensed that and took over. I will do the same for Helen and the boys." Mr. DeVere said.

"Mr. DeVere, I have known you for several years. Your family has served Goodland for over one hundred years. Didn't you get tired of people dying?" Max asked.

"You just used a word that sums up a funeral director that is worth his salt…SERVING,

I served this community for over sixty years. I missed thirty-one Christmas dinners, seventeen Easter dinners. We never went out on New Year's Eve because we were all on call. Even though cell phones, answering services and beepers came into our business, we still stayed home.

"I made fourteen removals on New Year's Eve, all but two drunk or hit by a drunk driver. When the town sleeps, I can get a death call and be up all night. I would have coffee with the boys at the local restaurant early that same morning.

"I'm not complaining. I loved every second of my life. When a service was over and a family member said that they were pleased… well that was all it took. It's like seventeen miserable holes of golf and making a thirty-foot putt on eighteen.

"I once had a fellow funeral director I tell me he was to the point that he hated to make removals and to embalm. He even hoped when the phone rang, that it would not be a death call. He asked my advice on what to do, or if it gets better.

"I told him to go to the hardware store and purchase the largest 'For Sale' sign they had and put it in the front yard of your funeral home. A few years later, he sold the funeral business and became a school teacher.

"Your friend Wally always displayed the utmost in professionalism. Several years ago, I had a body and called Wally to help me. He was on vacation, I later found out, but he came. We worked together for three days and I was so pleased with this young man, comforting the families from his heart. His energy and love for the funeral business was refreshing.

"Old man Tower did not pay Wally near what he was worth. Shortly before I sold my funeral home to Wally, Tower's son finished Mortuary school, a three year program, accomplished in five. I remember when Wally finished helping me those three days, I paid him. I paid him what he made in a month at Towers. Wally told me it was too much. I told him give it to his lovely wife. He smiled and thanked me. He came back the next morning and washed and waxed all of my vehicles.

"The DeVere Funeral Home is worth ten times what I sold it to Wally for. Helen will be comfortable for the rest of her life. The boys will have a good education. Helens heart will be empty though. Again, Max, I will be honored to take Wally into my care.

Max sat in his leather chair behind his desk. He stared at a picture on his wall of Wally and him with large cigars in their mouths, grinning from ear to ear. The picture was taken in Cancun.

Max got out of his chair and walked into his secretary's office.

"Cancel all of my appointments. Call Teresa and tell her to pack an overnight bag for the two of us. Don't look at me that way, like I'm crazy or something. I want to spend some time with my wife. Is that OK with you?" Max said in a gruff voice.

"Yes, Max, I will call your wife. You do have a heart beneath all of your toughness," she said with a weak smile.

"Well, don't tell anyone. Let's keep that our little secret, OK?" he said as he walked out of the office.

Vince Bowen went to the hospital to make the hardest removal of his career, his friend and mentor. He parked in the rear of the hospital. He was dressed in a sport coat, slacks and a nice conservative tie. He always believed his friend; Wally was right when he preached the importance of appearance. He approached the nurse's station and said he was there to take Wally into his care.

"Would you like some help with Wally, I will be happy to help you Mr. Bowen." The young nurse said holding back the tears. There was not a dry eye, nor a smile at the desk.

"No, that's not necessary, but thank-you." Vince said with a forced smile.

They gave him the paper work as he expressed his deepest sorrow to the nurses. Vince took his cot down to the basement to remove his friend. It was cold and quiet as emptiness came upon him. He wheeled his cot into the morgue and stood and looked at Wally on the stainless steel table, with a drape over his body. Someone at the hospital had draped Wally's body out of respect. Usually they were not covered.

Vince stood over his friend and wept. He wiped the tears away and he still could not believe that his friend was gone.

Vince positioned the cot next to the table. He slid Wally onto his cot. When he touched Wally, a wonderful feeling filled his heart. He closed his eyes and saw…

The End.